Eulogy for a Brown Angel

A Mystery Novel

Lucha Corpi

Arte Publico Press
Houston
Texas
1992

This book is made possible through a grant from the National Endowment for the Arts, a federal agency.

Arte Publico Press
University of Houston
Houston, Texas 77204-2090

Cover design by Mark Piñón

Lucha Corpi, 1945–
    Eulogy for a brown angel: a mystery novel / by Lucha Corpi.
        p.   cm.
    ISBN 1-55885-050-3
    I. Title
PS3553.0693E93 1992
813'.54–dc20   91-48072

                                                              CIP

The paper used in this publication meets the requirements of the American National Standard for Permanence of Paper for Printed Library Materials Z39.48-1984. ∞

For the past three years, *Eulogy* has been the reason, or the excuse, for my absent-mindedness, insecurity, idiosyncracy, and for the absence of nightmares often present during any other periods of intense prose writing. This goes to show that a little murder on paper can, and will, do wonders for one's sleep.

Although writing is an individual act, the editing and publishing of a book involves the work of many people. I wish then to thank those who have generously given me their expertise and energy—and funds—to make the writing and editing of this novel possible.

My heartfelt gratitude to the staff at the Oakland History Room and to Elissa Miller, Director of the Latin American Library, Oakland Public Library; to Louise Muhler for a most enjoyable lesson in horticulture; to Yolanda García Reyna for helping me understand the history and dynamics of L.A. gangs; to José and Malaquías Montoya for their permission to quote from or refer herein to their work; to Francisco Alarcón, Mark Greenside, Ted and Pee Wee Kalman, James Opiat, Alcides and Catherine Rodríguez-Nieto for their feedback at different stages of the early version of this book.

Special thanks to the Oakland Cultural Arts Commission for the fellowship that allowed me to take time off from teaching to finish the manuscript; and to my editor Roberta Fernández for the energy and work she has put into the final shaping of the book.

L.C.
Oakland, 1991

A la familia Corpi en México,
a mi hijo Arturo y a su esposa Naomi
y a Carlos Gonzales

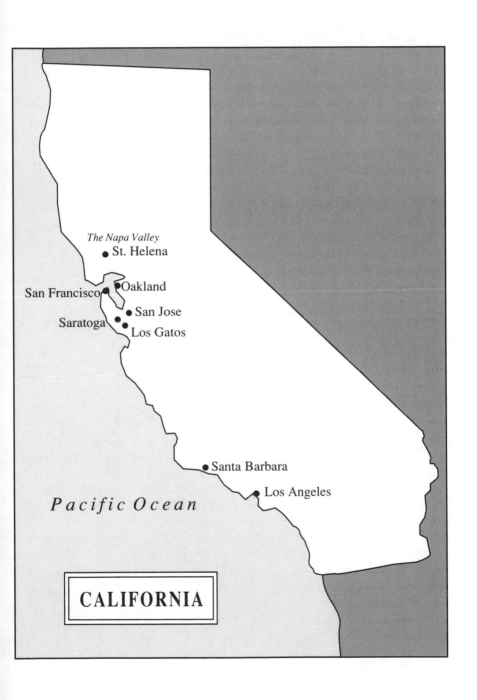

The Napa Valley
● St. Helena

San Francisco ●Oakland

Saratoga ● San Jose
● Los Gatos

● Santa Barbara

● Los Angeles

Pacific Ocean

CALIFORNIA

From the corrido "Garbanzo Beret" by José E. Montoya:

Por la Calle Whittier La Raza marchaba
En protesta del gobierno
con puños alzados, unidos gritaban
Que viva el poder del Chicano.

El Parque Lagunas parecía una fiesta
Una fiesta de colores.
Quien iba a pensar que esa tarde de amores
Se convirtiera en horrores.

◇   ◇   ◇

Down Whittier, La Raza marched
To protest against the government.
Fists raised, in one voice
they all chanted: Power to the Chicano!

Laguna Park looked like a fairground,
A celebration of color
Who would have thought that an afternoon
of love would later turn to horror.

Eulogy for a Brown Angel

A Mystery Novel

Prelude

For many years, every so often, I would sense the shimmering energy of a presence, somewhere at a distance. It came to me in the shape of a blue light, with a revolving force all its own. Once, while I was shopping at Union Square in San Francisco, I felt that presence, like a sudden gust of blue light brushing my arm and swiftly moving away. I didn't know it then, but it was *your* energy, Justin Escobar, I was feeling. I shivered, not in horror but in excitement, for I sensed that you and I would meet one day; and when we did, the solution to this mystery would be near at hand. Now, let me tell you the story.

1970
PART ONE

ONE

City of Angels

Luisa and I found the child lying on his side in a fetal position. He was about four years old, with curly, soft brown hair falling over his forehead, and partly covering his brows and long lashes. Small, round and still showing those tiny dimples that baby fat forms around the joints, his left hand rested on his head. He was wearing a Mickey Mouse watch on his wrist, marking 3:39 in the afternoon. Four minutes ahead of mine. His right arm partly covered his face, pulling his T-shirt up over the roundness of an over-sized liver. A soft, sleeping, brown cherub, so like my daughter Tania, probably napping back home at that very moment.

As the image of my daughter asleep in her bed surfaced so did the suspicion that something was very wrong. How could a child be asleep on a sidewalk off Whittier Boulevard in East Los Angeles? Had he gotten separated from his parents during the disturbance, then cried himself to sleep amid the popping and hissing of exploding gas canisters a few hundred feet away from us?

For two hours, we had been hearing the screams and cries of adults and children as they ran from the gas and the shattering of storewindows. There seemed to be no end in sight to the violence.

It was August 29, 1970, a warm, sunny Saturday that would be remembered as the National Chicano Moratorium, one of the most violent days in the history of California. Young and old, militant and conservative, Chicano and Mexican-American, grandchild and grandparent, Spanish-speaking and English-speaking, *vato loco* and college teacher, man and woman, all 20,000 of us had marched down Whittier Boulevard in the heart of the barrio. From as far north, west and east as Alaska, Hawaii and Florida, respectively, we had come to protest U.S. intervention in Southeast Asia and the induction of hundreds of young Chicanos into the armed forces. Laguna Park had been our gathering spot.

With our baskets of food, and our children, our poets, musicians,

17

leaders and heroes, we had come to celebrate our culture and reaffirm our rights to freedom of expression and peaceful assembly as Americans of Mexican descent.

In our idealism, Luisa and I, and others like us, hoped then that the police would appreciate our efforts to keep the demonstration peaceful and would help us maintain order with dignity. Surely, we thought, they would realize that we would not needlessly risk the lives of our very old and our very young. How foolish we had been. When a few of the marchers became disorderly, they were subdued by police officers in a brutal manner. People gathered around them and protested the officers' use of undue restraint. A bystander threw a bottle at the police, and five hundred officers armed with riot equipment marched against us. Our day in the sun turned into the bloody riot we were now running from.

I looked at the child again, at the unnatural stillness of that small body bathed in the afternoon sunlight, then felt Luisa's hand on my arm, pulling me away from him. Freeing myself I walked over to the child, hoping all the while that he was asleep or perhaps only slightly injured.

As I bent over, reaching out with a trembling hand to shake him, I became aware of the strong smell of excrement coming from him. Automatically, I pulled up the leg of his shorts and looked in. He was soiled, but not enough to account for such a strong smell. A fly swooped down and landed on his right arm, then another. Resisting the desire to fan them away from him, I watched as they raced over and under his elbow to his mouth, and with a trembling hand I lifted his arm. I was shaking violently by the time I saw the human excrement in his mouth.

I don't know that I understood entirely then what I had just uncovered, but when I realized that the child was dead and his body so defiled, I felt a jolt moving from my chest to the back of my neck, then to my stomach. With my eyes closed I felt my way to the wall. No sooner did I reach it than a burning wave of horror and impotent anger shoot up from my stomach and out of my mouth. My body went limp and I fell down in my own vomit, my eyes wide open. For an instant, I felt that I was looking down at the child, at Luisa and at myself from a place up above while the action below me rushed, like an old film, over a screen.

I felt I was floating over the rooftops. In the distance, clouds of teargas rose and mingled with the smoke of a dozen fires burning out of control. The fumes quickly overtook the crowds who then rushed onto the nearest streets that fanned out from Whittier Boulevard.

Two older people were hosing the teargas off the faces of passersby, among them several eighth-grade students and their teachers who were running towards a school bus. Two teenagers helped a third one, whose leg was bleeding profusely. Over their shoulders or cradled in their arms, some parents carried their children who had been overpowered by the gas fumes.

Policemen and sheriff's deputies armed with riot equipment marched against the crowds, using their batons to strike anyone who crossed their path or dared to strike back. Then they cuffed and filed them into the paddywagons.

Downtown, brown and black men gazed on the world through the reeky mist of alcohol, while beyond, in Beverly Hills, people gracefully slid in and out of stores on Rodeo Drive, then into chauffeured Roll Royces, Mercedes or Cadillacs. They headed down palm-lined streets towards their mansions, where their dark-skinned domestic staff tended to their every need.

On the horizon, a thin blue layer of haze marked the place where the Pacific Ocean, indifferent to the affairs of men, had met the land indefatigably every instant of every day since time immemorial.

I looked down at myself. There I was—all one hundred five pounds, five feet-four inches of me—lying fragile next to the dead boy, my dark skin glistening with sweat. How did I get up here? I wondered.

Luisa had her hands on my shoulders and was shouting my name again and again. Despite my desire to stay where I was, I began to descend and suddenly, I was holding on to her hands. I looked into her worried eyes and struggled to stand up.

Surely at least an hour had passed, I thought, as I collected myself and looked again at the dead boy with a coolheadedness that surprised me. I glanced at my watch: 3:45.

"Let's find a phone," I said.

"A phone? My God. Let's get out of here! You just scared the hell out of me. You looked dead, too." Luisa was pulling me by the arm. "There's nothing we can do for him." Her voice trembled and she cleared her throat, pretending to be tough, although I knew she was as affected by the death of the boy as I was. "They're getting closer. Listen," she warned.

I shook my head. "We're too far out of the way. They won't come here. At any rate, I can't just leave him here. You go on. I'll meet you at your house later."

Luisa began to walk away, then changed her mind and faced me. "Okay," she said, in resignation. She pointed in the direction opposite the Boulevard. "My friends Reyna y Joel Galeano live about two blocks from here. Remember I introduced you to them outside the *La Causa Chicana* newspaper yesterday? Joel is a freelance reporter." I nodded and Luisa added, "I'm sure you can call from their house. Go to the corner and turn right, go another two blocks, then left. It's the only blue house, the second one on your right. Number 3345, I think. I'll wait for you here."

"What if they're not home?" I asked.

"I'm sure Reyna is home. She told me she wasn't going to the march. She says she's terrified of crowds. Go on," Luisa commanded. "I'll watch over him." I turned in the direction she was pointing.

As soon as I rang the bell at the blue house, Reyna Galeano looked out the window; recognizing me, she opened the door. Joel was on the phone in the breakfast nook, and seemed to be dictating a news report.

"Joel just came in, too," Reyna told me, as she invited me to wait in the living room. "Rubén Salazar is hurt. He may even be dead. We don't know for sure." There were tears in her eyes.

"Who is Rubén Salazar?" I asked.

"He's a reporter for the *L.A. Times*. We just saw him yesterday. Joel talked to him about taking photos of the march for the paper."

"Oh yeah, now I know who he is. He also works for one of the Spanish-speaking TV stations here in L.A., doesn't he?" I sat down and looked at Reyna. "What happened to him?"

"We don't exactly know, but he was probably shot. At the Silver Dollar Cafe, where La Verne Street dead ends—oh, my God! I didn't mean to put it that way. Joel just came in and he's trying to get the facts."

"That's only a few blocks from here," I murmured. My legs itched and I started to scratch as I quickly considered and dismissed any possible connection between the shooting of Rubén Salazar and the death of the child. "We just found a little boy a couple of blocks from here," I said to Reyna. "He's dead. I came to call the police."

"You found a dead boy on the street?" Reyna looked incredulously at me. "I'm so glad our kids Mario and Vida are at my mother's in Santa Monica. We figured it was better not to have the children around today. From what you're saying, we were right."

Before I could answer Reyna's quick questions, I saw that Joel had finished with the phone, and I rushed to pick it up. "Sorry, don't mean to be rude but I need to call the police," I explained, then added, "I don't know if you remember me. I'm a friend of Luisa's."

"I remember you." He looked concerned. "Is it about Rubén Salazar?"

"No. I just found out about him from Reyna."

"I really don't think you should be calling the pigs. We're almost sure one of them shot Rubén."

"This isn't about him," I interrupted. "It's about a little boy Luisa and I just found." I wasn't making sense, yet I knew that groping for words and getting the sequence of events right was going to take too long. Joel raised his eyebrows but he didn't question me further. He sat at the table and began to go over his notes.

I dialed "information," then hesitated. Should I call the homicide division? I was very sure I had found a murder victim, but I dialed the general information number anyway.

Since I was rambling on about finding a little boy dead on the sidewalk in the vicinity of Whittier Boulevard, I kept getting transferred from one section to another of the L.A.P.D. I had been reluctant to mention the excrement in the child's mouth, afraid that I would not be taken seriously. "Somebody listen, please," I pleaded into the static at the other end of the line when I was put on hold once more.

Aware that Joel was giving me an "I-told-you-so" look, I tried avoiding his gaze and turned my attention to the photos and certificates on the wall in front of me. I could see he'd won a couple of awards for photos he'd taken in Viet Nam. I studied a photo of Joel in fatigues with other Marines until a voice came on the phone.

"This is Matthew Kenyon. I understand you have a matter for homicide?" Too late to worry now about having called the police. Joel frowned, shook his head, then left the kitchen.

"A child was murdered this afternoon, I tell you. I found him on the street with *shit* in his mouth. I mean that literally. *Shit!*" I said impatiently to this Matthew Kenyon, no doubt an old cop with a desk job, feeling sorry for himself for not being out there where he could get some action. Immediately, I felt ashamed for blurting out such a crude description of a child whose death had so profoundly disturbed me.

Ironically, it was the crudeness of my remark that made Matthew Kenyon take notice of what I had to say. As I found out soon thereafter Kenyon was a middle-aged detective in the homicide division who had purposely, I suspected after meeting him, not participated in the assault on the demonstrators at Laguna Park.

"What's your name?" he asked me. I hesitated. A Spanish surname always meant a delay of at least an hour in emergencies. He seemed to guess the reason for my hesitation and added, "All right. Just give me your first name."

"Okay," I answered, "my name is Gloria. Gloria Damasco."

"That's good, Gloria." There was no hint of pleasure or displeasure in his voice. "Are you related to the dead boy?"

"No. I just found him." I was losing patience.

"Yes. Now, tell me. Where exactly did you find the boy?"

"On Marigold Street, corner with Marguerite, a few blocks from Whittier Boulevard."

"Are you there now?"

"No. But I can meet you there."

"I'll be there in ten minutes. But I want you to do me a favor. Go back to the place where you found the boy and make sure no one touches him or anything around him."

As I put the receiver on the hook, I realized that somewhere in that city named after Our Lady of the Angels of Porciúncula, a killer roamed the streets or waited at home for news, the knowledge of his crime still fresh in his consciousness.

TWO

Insidious Disease

Little Michael David Cisneros had been identified by his mother and father, Lillian and Michael Cisneros, about six hours after Luisa and I found him. His maternal grandmother, Otilia Juárez, who had reported him missing at 2:45 that afternoon, claimed that he'd been taken from the porch of her house on Alma Avenue, about three blocks from Laguna Park.

We had found him less than two miles from Otilia Juárez's house, approximately the length of the area swept by the police during the riot as they forced the crowd from the park back towards Atlantic Park where the march had originated.

Joel had insisted on going back with me to that spot. Michael David's body was there, still with no more company than Luisa and the flies. I knelt down to fan them away so that Joel could take pictures of the scene. He didn't seem to have the same reaction I'd had when I first looked at the body, but his hands shook as he snapped photo after photo.

Luisa assured me that nothing had been disturbed. No one had passed by, for the area was quite isolated. A building rose to a height of about three floors on the side of the street where we stood. It was one of those windowless low-budget plaster fortresses where unwanted memories are stored and sometimes forgotten. Across the street, a number of small neighborhood stores had been closed because of the disturbance. Even under ordinary circumstances this was an out-of-the way street, a good ten blocks from the main thoroughfare.

Suddenly I saw a Chicano teenager standing at the corner, smoking a cigarette and glancing furtively in our direction. He was wearing a red bandana, folded twice and tied around his head, a black leather vest, no shirt, and black pants. Just then, he turned around and I noticed that a skull with a halo above it and the word "Santos" were painted on the back of his vest. He seemed no older than eighteen, most likely a "home boy," a member of a youth gang. What was he doing there, I wondered.

Luisa told us she'd seen him cross that intersection twice since she'd been there. It was obvious the young man didn't seem disturbed by our surveillance and, after a few minutes, he began to walk in our direction. Luisa instinctively retreated behind me, and I, behind Joel. Finding himself suddenly cast in the role of defender, Joel put his camera in its case and began searching his pockets for something to use as a weapon.

Two years before, after a couple of attempted rapes of students at Cal State Hayward, Luisa and I had taken a self-defense course for women and, as a reward for our good performance, we had received a small container of mace, a permit to carry it, and a whistle. I reached for the whistle and Luisa grabbed the mace from her purse. Seeing our weapons, Joel gave a sigh of relief. Then he frowned as though he recognized the young man.

"Is this guy someone you know?" I asked Joel. He shook his head.

With a slow stride, the young man approached, then stopped a few feet away from us.

"*Soy Mando,*" he said and looked straight at Joel, but his eyes took in everything between the wall and the opposite sidewalk. He threw a quick glance at the body, then at me. "*El chavalito este. ¿Es tuyo?*"

"No," I replied, "it's not my child." This Mando was much younger than he'd seemed from a distance, not quite fifteen. Not a bad young man either, I sensed, and relaxed a little.

"The dude who brought the *chavalito* here dropped this." Mando handed me a folded newspaper clipping which had turned yellow and was already showing signs of wear at the creases. No doubt it had been kept for a long time in a wallet.

My heart beat wildly and my hands shook as I reached for the clipping. Almost automatically, I closed my eyes. I suddenly sensed the presence of a man. I saw his shadow, then a small house surrounded by tall trees. Somewhere in the area children were laughing. The scene passed and I felt nauseous, but I managed to overcome the desire to vomit. Still I had to hold on to Luisa.

My strange behavior disconcerted her, but Mando didn't pay any heed to it. Perhaps he had witnessed stranger things, seen a lot of pain or wanton cruelty in his short life. I doubted there was much left in this world that would shake him, except perhaps the death of the child. Why had he decided to give *us* the clipping? And why did I trust him? Instinctively I felt he had nothing to do with the death of the child.

"Did you see the person who did this? Can you tell us what he looked like?" Joel took a small memo pad and pencil from his shirt pocket, flipping for a blank page. Like my husband, who was also left-handed, Joel held the memo pad in the hollow of his right hand, across his chest.

"I didn't see nothing. Understand? *Nada.*" Mando looked at Joel's hand, put his palms out, and took a couple of steps back.

"How do we know it wasn't you who killed this *chicanito*?" There was a double edge of contempt and defiance in Joel's voice, which surprised both Luisa and me.

Mando stood his ground across from us. His eyes moved rapidly from Joel's face to his torso and arms, locking on the camera hanging from his neck. A wry smile began to form on Mando's lips. He spat on the ground, wiped his mouth with the back of his hand. "Later, *vato,*" he said, waving a finger at Joel.

"*Cuando quieras,*" Joel answered back, accepting the challenge. "Any time," he repeated.

Irritated with their childish confrontation, Luisa commanded, "Stop it! Both of you!" She looked at Joel, then added, "A child is dead. That's why we're here."

Joel's face flushed with anger, but he remained quiet. Mando turned slightly to the left, cocking his head. The only noise was the distant clattering of the waning riot. Mando moved close to me and whispered in my ear, "The dude—the one who brought the *chavalito*? He wasn't a member of the Santos. I know 'cause he was wearing a wig. *Era gabacho.* He had a scar, a *media luna*, a half-moon on his right arm."

Looking over his right shoulder, Mando began moving swiftly down the street, every muscle in his body ready for either attack or defense. I was fascinated, yet sad. A mother would be crying for him sooner than later, I thought. Not many gang members live long enough to bury their mothers.

"I'll see if I can get some more information from him," Joel said. He ran off in pursuit of Mando, who was already turning the corner when Matthew Kenyon's unmarked car stopped with a screech beside us.

Why is it that cops and tough men, young or old, have to brake or start up a car with a screech, I wondered. Do they think they are establishing turf, like moose or sea elephants?

I looked towards the corner. How had Mando known the cops were on their way? I had a feeling I would never have a chance to ask him.

So I gave my full attention to Kenyon. He was a lanky man, six feet tall, with very short red hair already graying and a pallid, freckled face. Everything seems to be fading in this man, I thought, as I focused on his Roman nose, his only feature that seemed atypical.

With Kenyon was another man who answered to the name of Todd, obviously from the crime lab since he was already marking the place where the body lay. A third man, driving a car marked with the seal of the Los Angeles County Coroner's Office, pulled up behind Kenyon's car. He, too, got out and began to examine the body.

Before questioning us, Kenyon helped Todd cordon off the area. Actually, he hardly paid any attention to us at all until Todd referred to the vomit on the sidewalk and I claimed it as mine.

"Ah, yes. Gloria Damasco?" Kenyon said. It amazed me that anyone besides Marlon Brando and Humphrey Bogart could speak without moving his upper lip in the slightest. True, it is easier to do that in English than in Spanish, because of the closeness in quality of English vowels; but Kenyon's case, next to Brando's and Bogie's, was definitely one for the books. He had soulful, expressive eyes, and perhaps because of that I expected his voice to reveal much more emotion.

"Yes," I said, "I'm Gloria Damasco."

I asked Luisa for the clipping Mando had given us and was about to hand it to Kenyon when I was seized by the same kind of fear I had felt when I had tried to take it from Mando earlier. Again, I saw the house, but this time I saw the word "park" carved into a board next to it. In my haste to get rid of the clipping before I became nauseated again, I threw it at the policeman. "Here. I think the murderer might have dropped this."

"So much for fingerprints," Todd muttered, shaking his head.

"I told you not to disturb anything." Despite his perfectly controlled tone, Kenyon's eyes showed anger, but I didn't care since I was more preoccupied with the realization that I was experiencing something out of the ordinary every time I touched that clipping. Perhaps it was only the product of what my grandmother called my "impressionable mind," her term for an imagination that could easily develop a morbid curiosity for the forbidden or the dark side of nature. Even a liking for death. These possibilities distressed me.

I must have looked pretty distraught because Kenyon invited Luisa and me to wait in his car. Since he had already taken note of our names and addresses perhaps he simply wanted us out of the way until he had time to question us, I thought.

We got into the back seat and I lowered the window so I could hear what Todd and the Coroner were telling Kenyon, who was now putting Michael David's body on a stretcher and covering him with a cloth. "Well, Dr. D., was he strangled?"

Dr. D., whose full name, according to his tag, was Donald Dewey, nodded, then shook his head, making the detective raise an eyebrow. "Whoever did this wanted to be extra sure the boy would die. So the boy was drugged. I'm almost sure. This is all preliminary, you know. I'll have more for you in the morning."

"That soon?" Kenyon smiled. "They're putting the others in the deep freeze, huh?" He flipped the pages in his notebook and read aloud: "Rubén Salazar, Angel Díaz and Lynn Ward."

"Looks that way." Dr. Dewey picked up his equipment and headed towards the coroner's wagon. "Just buying time, I suppose. They got themselves into a real jug of *jalapeño* this time." I wondered if "they" referred to the police or to the demonstrators. Dr. Dewey came back after putting everything in the vehicle, then called Kenyon aside.

Trying not to be too conspicuous, I stuck my head out the window but I could hear only fragments of the conversation since both men were speaking in a low voice. " ... Second opinion. You never know. You'll have to tell them ... soon." Dr. Dewey patted Kenyon on the shoulder.

"Maybe Joel was right," I concluded. "Maybe it was a mistake to call the cops."

"Someone was going to do it anyway," Luisa said in a reassuring tone.

Todd and Kenyon picked up the stretcher and headed towards the wagon.

"Before I forget," Kenyon said to the coroner. "Will you find out as much as you can about the fecal matter?"

"Try my best," Dr. Dewey answered. "Need about two weeks, though." He shook his head. "Real backlog and two lab boys just went on vacation." Kenyon nodded and waved at the coroner.

I made the sign of the cross, closed my eyes and said a silent prayer for the dead child. My eyes were burning inside my lids. I opened them again and looked at my watch. It was now 5:15. The sun was still beating down on the streets and the sirens of ambulances and patrol cars were still wailing in the distance.

I had aged years in just a few hours. By sundown, I would be as old as Mando.

For Rubén Salazar, Angel Gilberto Díaz, and Lynn Ward there was no going home, and the horror that would make the living toss and turn for many nights was of little consequence to them now. They were lying on autopsy slabs, side by side, waiting for their bodies to be opened and drained of blood, their insides emptied, then studied and tested to determine the exact cause of death.

In time, perhaps someone would admit to the *real* cause of what happened that day. But perhaps we already knew the name of the insidious disease that had claimed three, perhaps four, more lives that late August afternoon.

More than ever before, I wanted to go home, to hold my daughter and seek the comfort of Darío's arms. But the spirit of the dead child had taken hold of me. I would no longer be able to go about my life without feeling his presence in me.

THREE

Optical Illusions

Night finally came, restoring peace of a sort to that bloody Saturday. It let those wounded in flesh as well as spirit go home and begin the healing process.

It was about eleven o'clock when we got to Luisa's apartment. Until two months ago, she had lived in Oakland but once she received notification of admittance as a graduate student to U.C.L.A., she had moved to Los Angeles, wanting to get settled before classes began.

Joel had been kind enough to pick us up outside the L.A.P.D., where we'd spent the last five hours as reluctant guests of Matthew Kenyon.

The evening mist had moved inland from the ocean. By the time we left, the mist was already condensing enough to release its moisture at the slightest contact with a cold wind. I welcomed it.

Something over which I didn't seem to have any control was working in me or around me. I sensed it the moment we walked out of the police department into the wet evening. A glimmer, a smattering of a presence, of someone out there, waiting for me, raised the hair on my arms.

It did not fill me with fear or horror. The rational part of me told me this sensation had to be simply the manifestation of an overloaded nervous system. We were carrying a layer of dry sweat, teargas and dust on us like a second skin and our souls were burdened with the sediment of the frustration and anger that results from a confrontation with violence.

Luisa and I each showered as soon as we arrived at her apartment. She was so tired she did not eat dinner, and she went to bed immediately. As a matter of fact, neither of us had had any food since that morning. My stomach, like my mouth, felt raw.

I'd answered every question Kenyon had asked about our activities during the Moratorium. Luisa and I had reviewed every detail related to our discovery of little Michael's body and the brief conversation with Mando. Joel had not been able to catch up with Mando, so we had no information about how he'd discovered the murdered child.

During the interrogation, I didn't have an inkling about what Kenyon was considering. I had sensed, however, that he'd been caught between two possibilities. Either I'd been telling him the truth and this Mando of the Santos gang really existed. Or I had been hiding something because I really knew who the murderer was but was protecting him or her. Either way, Kenyon had advised me to stay in town for two or three days in case he needed to talk to me again or to identify Mando if they caught up with him.

I drank a tall glass of cold milk while I called Darío in Oakland, to let him know I was all right. He was a resident physician at Merritt Hospital, and his shift was over at nine in the evening on Saturdays. By now, he would have picked up Tania at my mother's, and my daughter would have been in bed for hours.

"She wants Mommy to come home with the Bugs Bunny you promised her," Darío told me. I sensed from his voice that he had already heard about the disturbance at the Moratorium and had been very worried, but didn't reproach me for not calling earlier.

I shrank from the prospect of having to go over everything again. Fortunately, the late evening news had featured parts of the riot and the death of Rubén Salazar, and I only talked to Darío briefly about the march. Then I told him about my discovering the child's body and relayed Kenyon's request that I stay in town for a few days. Before hanging up, I promised him I'd be at my job interview at the speech clinic at Herrick Hospital on Thursday. Yes, I would call collect every night, and yes, I would take care of myself. I purposely didn't mention any of my "flying" experiences. I suppose I felt embarrassed since I had always sought rational explanations for anything that happened to me, using intuition to support reason rather than the other way around.

After a long day of dragging around a psyche gone amuck, with only rage and fear as ballast, I now felt I was drifting into what I could only describe as neurotic lucidity. Sitting up in the darkness, unable to go to sleep, I had a sense that I was looking at two sides of myself as if on a photographic negative—the lighter areas being "reality"; the darker shades of colors, even perhaps the absence of color, being optical illusions.

A similar illusion had been at work in Mando's description of the person who had carried little Michael's body to the street, where we'd found him. Thinking it over, I concluded that whoever had moved the body had been purposefully dressed like the Santos.

Mando must have had his reasons for waiting around, perhaps knowing I would be back, preferably before the police arrived. It occurred to me then that Mando had probably spotted the individual wearing a Santos vest, and had followed that person to the place where we had found little Michael. He must have managed to get close enough to notice the scar and the man's wig. It stood to reason then that he also knew the color of the man's eyes, his build and height. But how had Mando managed to see so much without being seen himself? Was it safe to assume that the man with the wig—assuming that Mando was right and the Santos' impersonator was a man—was also little Michael's killer? Yes, I told myself, it was one and the same. My own certainty scared me.

Perhaps Mando and the rest of the Santos were looking at that very moment for the individual who'd impersonated one of them. Perhaps, for Mando that was all that mattered—his and the gang's honor. Yet, Mando could obviously have gone after the Santos' impersonator; he could even have killed him, but had not. No doubt he hadn't acquired a taste for death. So instead, Mando stopped to check on little Michael. Like me, he must have gone through the shock of discovering the excrement in the child's mouth, then waited for someone else to find the body. He must have picked up the newspaper clipping and, hoping for a clue to the killer's identity, must have read it.

I realized this train of thought might be leading me on to yet another deception. I had to believe that Mando hadn't lost all sensitivity, that he had experienced the same horror I had at the sight of the shit in little Michael's mouth.

In the meantime, the killer had probably sought the anonymity offered by the disorder and confusion of the riot. My intuition (and I would use that word very carefully from that day forward) told me that this was no ordinary killer. It couldn't be a kidnapping gone awry, as Luisa had suggested, because kidnappers would have kept the body until they had collected the ransom. No. This murderer must have had access to the kind of information he needed to formulate his plan and then execute it.

Kenyon had told Luisa and me that the boy's parents, Michael and Lillian Cisneros, lived in the San Francisco Bay Area, and that they'd come to L.A. specifically to attend the Moratorium march. Since little Michael had been taken from his grandmother's house, his abductor had to know both her address and the surrounding area. That person also had to be aware of the route chosen for the march, and maybe even the size of the police force that would be used to confront the marchers.

Joel had told me he suspected a policeman had killed little Michael. At that point, with such little evidence, almost anything was possible; however, a particular detail nagged me. The killer had planted the excrement in Michael David's mouth. Was it his own private joke, perhaps, or his calling card? And if so, for whom was it intended? What was his reason for killing a child? Obviously I didn't have all the information I needed to walk this through my mind, but perhaps Mando could give me a fuller description of the murderer and clarify some other details for me.

I felt revulsion and anger rising up in me once more and closed my eyes. To my surprise I heard the laughter of children again, then I saw tall pine trees, a few picnic tables and a house. A wooden sign with "park" written on it was visible a hundred feet away. If only I could get closer to the sign and see the rest of it, I would know which park I was looking at, I thought. I began moving but not towards the sign. Instead, I climbed up a small hill towards an area where the children were playing, and I could hear their laughter and chatter getting closer. Then an older man's loud voice began calling for Michael. Now, I could see the little boy's back. He was standing next to a Spanish pine in the yard of a house, but this was definitely not the house in or near the park.

When the scene faded, I opened my eyes. Surely there was a connection between the clipping and this array of images triggered in my imagination every time I thought about the clipping. What was the significance of its contents, I wondered as I turned on the light and got up to get my purse?

I pulled out the copy of the clipping I had requested from Kenyon. Someone had scribbled *January 10, 1947* at the top of the article. The name of the newspaper didn't appear anywhere, but the information in the article referred to a Cecilia Castro-Biddle. The woman was claiming to be a descendant of the Peralta family, who under Spanish and then Mexican rule had owned a land grant the size of five large cities across the bay from San Francisco.

Luisa had laughed when we first had looked at the clipping, for it was clear that the writer had had an ax to grind with Mrs. Castro-Biddle for claiming a link to the historically important Peralta family and was trying to put her in her place.

I hadn't a clue as to how the content of the newspaper clipping related to the murder of little Michael Cisneros, I decided, then went back to bed.

I closed my eyes and began to fall asleep. I wanted to pray but all I could say was: "God, may it all have been a nightmare." Then, on some subconscious second thought, I added: "But if it wasn't, let me find the solution to this puzzle. Point the way."

Laughing at the ambivalence of my prayer, I felt myself rising again, joined by a silver thread to a little boy who watched in fascination as our shared umbilical cord wound around the Spanish pine between us.

FOUR

A Mother's Pool of Tears

From the street, there was nothing singular about Otilia Juárez's house. It was a one-story stucco. Except for the large, black satin bow that now hung from the front gate, it was similar to many other houses in the neighborhood. A chain-link fence surrounded the front lawn. Red geraniums bloomed along the fence.

Once past the gate, Luisa and I noticed the two features that distinguished the house from the others. A willow-oak, a sinuous tree more natural to the East Coast than to East Los Angeles, stood beside a wide porch where Mexican pots on pedestals held flowering peonies, daisies, and carnations. A marble fountain in the shape of the *Pietà* stood beside the tree. I imagined water spurting out of the two small holes under the mother's eyes, cascading down, bathing the body of the Son on its way to the small receptacle below. The water in the basin looked clean and was probably kept that way for the benefit of the birds, and the children.

I was beginning to become sentimental again, so I hurried to the front porch. Otilia Juárez must have heard the gate close because she stepped out onto the porch. Behind her, a young man stuck his head out the door but, as soon as he saw us, he went back into the house. One of the Juárez children, Luisa and I speculated.

"We've come to pay our respects," Luisa said. I nodded. Mrs. Juárez greeted us, then invited us into her living room. I assumed that the young man had disappeared behind one of the closed doors.

Despite our polite refusal, she insisted on making coffee and preparing something sweet for us. It was obvious that our acknowledgment of her family's loss had already made us deserving of every courtesy in her home.

Even under the most tragic of circumstances, women of Otilia Juárez's generation would put their own grief aside and see to the comfort of those who suffered around them. Perhaps it was their way of not letting their own emotions run them aground. As long as they were dealing with somebody else's feelings, their own were kept in check until such time as they could cope with them.

Looking at Otilia, I found myself thinking about my mother. At that moment, I would have indeed welcomed her arms around me. Sensing my vulnerability, I suddenly began to feel uncomfortable about being there. Hadn't Matthew Kenyon warned me the night before against visiting little Michael's family?

"Don't do it," he had said. "For their sake and yours, too." He had fixed his eyes on me, waiting for a promise, but I wouldn't give it. "Suit yourself," he said.

Later in the evening Kenyon had touched on the subject again, saying in his non-emphatic tone, "You'll have to explain why you're there to see them, and you'll have to tell them what you know about this mess. Leave the explaining and the investigation to me. That's my job."

Maybe he was right; but he was wrong in assuming that curiosity could be my only motive for seeking a meeting with Lillian Cisneros' mother. Neither of us realized then how much I *needed* to share my grief with the family, to have them tell me that everything was going to be all right. I straightened up and, as I did so, all the tension, confusion and anger from the day before seemed to have concentrated on my lower back which had ached all morning long. Sadness too had been swelling inside me, pushing against my eyelids. It took every ounce of the little energy I had left to keep the storm from breaking.

To ease the ache in my back and to get my mind on something else, I got up and walked around the living room. The room was spacious, with sheer curtains on the front windows and a polished wood floor partially covered with a large gray, brown and blue striped sarape rug.

People in Jingle Town, the Mexican barrio around the Del Monte Cannery where I grew up in Oakland, would have accused us of "wanting to be more gringo than the gringos themselves" if we had put a Mexican sarape on the floor instead of on the bed. I smiled. Mariquita Montes and Lucía Rosendo, my mother's best friends and *comadres*, would definitely consider the rug in Otilia's house "un-Mexican." Other parts of the house would pass the test though: the porcelain figurines, the Sacred Heart statuette, the votive candles, the silk and crepe paper flowers, the framed image of the Virgin of Guadalupe, the family pictures on the wall.

I began to look at the photographs. In one of them I recognized the young man who had come to the door when we arrived. Since I'd had a brief glimpse of Michael and Lillian Cisneros when Kenyon took them to the Coroner's Office to identify their son, I recognized them in one of the photos. It was the usual picture of the bride and groom with the other members of the wedding party. Otilia was standing between Lillian and another young woman I assumed was the maid of honor. At Michael Cisneros' side stood a tall older man in tails, and next to him, a man with blondish hair. He looked only slightly younger than the groom and was the only one in the group not smiling. There was a faint resemblance between him and the older man. For some reason, all three men seemed vaguely familiar.

Otilia walked back into the living room with a tray. Luisa immediately set aside the porcelain figurines on the coffee table to make room for the tray.

"They were taken five years ago," Otilia said in a steady but raspy voice, as she saw me looking at the wedding photos. "Michael's father died two years after the wedding, almost to the day." Her hands were shaking lightly and the coffee cups rattled.

Taking the cup from her, I was relieved that we were not talking about the death of her grandson.

"Mr. Cisneros had a heart condition," she went on, "which got worse after his wife, Karen, passed away. We didn't know her, but Michael and his brother Paul have always said that she was a wonderful woman."

I looked at Otilia as she talked. Her hair was pulled straight back and gathered in a bun. Although she didn't have any loose strands, she repeatedly passed her hand over her hair to smooth it.

The conversation was taking the wrong turn, I feared. No doubt she had already suffered many losses in her life, and now she had probably experienced the worst one of all. In a glance I saw that many of the photos were of little Michael and I figured that he was her only grandchild, for no other youngsters appeared in any of the photos.

Hoping to change the conversation, I asked Otilia, "Who is the young man standing next to Michael's father in the wedding picture?"

"That's Paul, Michael's younger brother. He favors his mother. Karen was Swedish, tall and blonde," she said pensively.

"I guess Michael looks more like his father," Luisa commented. On the other hand, little Michael looked more like Lillian, I thought, but kept the comparison to myself.

Otilia looked up at the wedding photo. "Michael has been trying to reach Paul, who's been in Germany for four weeks, doing some work for the company. When their father died, the two sons took over the family business. Perhaps you've heard of it—the Black Swan Enterprises, Inc., up north, in Oakland?"

"Yes, I have," I said. I realized where it was I had seen Michael and

Paul Cisneros' photo. As a successful company of Mexican-American ownership, Black Swan had recently been featured in the local section of *El Vocero de la Bahía*, a bilingual weekly newspaper.

"Are the Cisneros related to the Peralta family?" Luisa asked.

I gasped, making Luisa realize she had said the wrong thing.

Otilia looked at both of us and set her cup down. I had expected sooner or later she would get around to asking us how we knew about her grandson's death. Now the moment had come. It saddened me to think I would never be able to share in their grief nor they in mine, for I could never describe to them what I saw when Luisa and I found little Michael's body.

"That is the same question Detective Sergeant Kenyon asked us yesterday," she replied as she scrutinized us.

"Luisa and I discovered your grandson's body yesterday," I volunteered. Then, we all fell silent.

Finally, Luisa said in a quavering voice, "We wanted to come personally to express our sympathy." The pressure around my eyes worsened.

"I see," Otilia brushed her hair back with her automatic gesture.

"The tragic death of your grandson has touched us deeply," I tried to explain, but my eyelids were giving way to the pressure, and I had to pause. "Please believe me," I finally said.

I could see that Otilia did believe my words and sensed my need to be there. "Do you have any children?" she asked, trying to make me feel comfortable and to change the conversation.

"A girl, three years old." All I could think of asking was, "Is Lillian your youngest child?"

"No. Actually she's the oldest. My youngest, Victor, opened the door for you. I have two other daughters but Lillian has always looked younger than her sisters."

"How is she doing?"

Otilia was having a hard time keeping the tears back. Luisa had been quiet all this time and I decided to follow her example. Otilia said nothing for a while. The look in her eyes made me suspect that she was debating whether she should even talk to us any more. But her need to make sense of things proved to be greater than her caution or her stoicism because suddenly she began to talk about Lillian's childhood.

"When Lilly was ten years old, she came home with a book the librarian at school had given to her to read." Otilia spoke slowly, almost measuring the length of each word. "At that time, my husband was very sick," she continued. "He had cancer and the doctors had said he only had a few months to live. Every day, as soon as Lillian got home from school, she'd go into her father's room to read to him. One day she brought the book the librarian had given her. It was *Alice's Adventures in Wonderland.* During the next three weeks, she read a few pages from that book to him daily.

" 'It's a wonderful book,' he told her, 'the best we've read yet.' Then, after three weeks he developed pneumonia and we had to hospitalize him. He slipped into a coma, and even though we had told Lilly that her father couldn't hear her, she asked me to take her to the hospital so she could read to him again from their special book.

"She had barely begun her reading when my husband died. Lilly cried so much I had to ask the doctor to give her a tranquilizer. But, of course, as time passed, she seemed to get over her father's death.

"Then one day, when she was twelve, we went to a place near the cemetery to order a headstone for my husband's grave. At the time, I had finally been able to get a good job and could afford payments on the stone. Lilly was immediately taken up with a fountain which depicted the weeping Mother and her Son dead at her feet."

"Yes, we saw it outside," Luisa said. "It's very unusual."

"Well," Otilia resumed her story, "Lilly asked the shop owner to lower his price considerably, and he did. When I asked her why she wanted to have that particular fountain, she told me, 'It has a pool of tears, Mami. Just like in the story I read to Papi before he died.' To tell you the truth, I couldn't see the connection. But of all my children, she was the one most affected by her father's death. She always seemed to associate his death with that fountain.

"Early this morning, Michael woke me up. 'Lilly was gone,' he said. We found her outside, lying on the ground next to the fountain. 'This is my pool of tears,' she kept saying. 'I'm going to drown in it. What have I done?' She's so heart-broken, yet she hasn't cried a single tear and that worries me a lot. I would prefer that she give in to her sorrow.

"Ever since she went to identify our little Michael's body, she has been asking the same question: 'What have I done? What have I done?' There's no way to convince her that none of us could predict what was going to happen. I had promised Lilly and Michael I would keep an eye on little Michael while they participated in the Moratorium march. So, if anyone is to blame, it's me for not putting the chain on the door to keep little Michael from getting out."

Otilia stopped. Luisa and I couldn't think of anything to say that would comfort her.

I felt my throat getting tight and cleared it. "Did he do that often?"

Otilia gave me a puzzled look. "What do you mean?"

"Did little Michael often open the door to go play on the lawn?"

"Not really," she said. "But he would run to the door as soon as someone knocked. Yesterday, while he was waiting for Lilly and Michael to come back, I was trying to get him used to looking out the window instead. I even left the curtains drawn a little." She stood up and walked to a door next to the kitchen. "I went into the bathroom but left the door open so I could hear him playing with his blocks and his cars. Then, in the brief time I took to flush the toilet and wash my hands, something happened. I came back here and immediately saw that the front door and gate were both open. Little Michael was gone."

"Was that when you called the police?" Luisa asked.

"No, I didn't call right away. First, I went looking for him in the yard, then around the block. After all, how far could a three-year-old go in just a few minutes?"

"Did you see any cars leaving the area?" I asked. "Perhaps you saw the person who took him, but didn't realize it at that moment."

Otilia shook her head and sat down on a chair by the window. "Detective Kenyon already asked me that and so many other questions. Do I know anyone who hates Michael? A business associate, maybe? Does anyone hate my daughter? Had I noticed any strangers roaming around the house the day before? Are any of us related to the Peralta family in Oakland? I'd have given an arm to be able to have said yes to any of his questions." She was breathing hard and her eyes were moist.

"Where is your daughter now?" I sat down beside her and put my arm around her shoulders.

"Lilly and Michael went to the police department. From there, they were going to the mortuary. We're taking my little Michael back to Oakland as soon as the police release him. That's where the funeral will take place."

I had hoped she would let go a little and cry, but she was determined not to do that.

"Mrs. Juárez ... "

"Please, call me Otilia. It's okay."

"Thank you. Would it be all right if we phone you ... sometime?" She nodded and I continued. "Luisa and I are both from Oakland, but she lives in L.A. now. I'm going back home soon."

"Please. I would very much like for you to call me."

Half an hour later, when Otilia's neighbors began to walk in to pay their respects, Luisa and I said goodbye. On the way out, I stopped to look at the fountain with its pool at the Madonna's feet. "*This is my pool of tears. What have I done?*" Lilly's words. An odd choice, I thought.

"I was really surprised that Otilia told us so much about Lillian," Luisa mused. "She seems so self-contained—and we *are* strangers."

"We all do odd things in tragic situations," I said, thinking about my "flying" experience the day before. "Besides, we both are good people, aren't we?"

Luisa didn't answer. Instead, she asked, "Do you believe in fate, Gloria?"

That same thought had crossed my mind earlier that morning. "I didn't until yesterday. Now ... I don't know. Do you?"

"I always have. I've never been rational like you." She laughed softly.

"Do we *really* have any control over anything in this world? Was this also fate's doing?" I asked as we crossed Laguna Park again, towards Whittier Boulevard. Luisa didn't answer.

The cleaning crews were already at work. Piles of clothing were strewn, still saturated with the smell of teargas and blood. Picnic gear, containers full of food and drinks were everywhere. We even saw a stroller and a baby rattle. Luisa and I looked straight ahead as if that way we could keep our hearts from racing, our minds from remembering.

Just for an instant I felt a glimmer of a presence watching me. He waited, perhaps for a propitious time, to come closer. I turned around slowly and scanned the park. At that moment, a shadow moved across the sun as it broke through the clouds.

FIVE

Shadows Behind the Altar

The church was almost deserted. I sat down on one of the pews at the rear of the nave, near the entrance. It was cool and peaceful, and that was nice; but best of all, I could be by myself for a short while.

I had left Luisa at the Galeanos' house, where the conversation centered around the death of Rubén Salazar, with everyone speculating about the events to come. Surely they would hold an inquest but how could anyone be trusted to tell the truth? This time the police had gone too far. After all, Rubén Salazar wasn't just any Chicano; he was a reporter and a TV news personality. The *Los Angeles Times* would definitely put pressure on the Internal Affairs Division of the L.A.P.D. to conduct a thorough and fair investigation.

Joel had led the discussion until Oscar Zeta Acosta, a Chicano writer and attorney, paid the group a visit. He was defending those arrested at the Moratorium and was looking for a journalist named Olivar from *La Causa Chicana*, an East L.A. newspaper.

I had been in the kitchen talking with Reyna and her mother, Sylvia Castañeda, who had driven in from Santa Monica with Reyna's and Joel's children. Sylvia and Reyna kept talking about money and how little of it there was in that house. "Ese huevón—good-for-nothing" was Sylvia's constant description of Joel. Reyna would defend Joel mildly but mostly she kept quiet.

Tired of witnessing this mother-daughter interaction and of hearing about injustice, violence, death and ambition so soon after our talk with Otilia, I felt in urgent need of solitude and rest.

Following Luisa's suggestion, I decided to visit Saint Augustine's Church, which was only a ten-minute walk from the Galeanos' house. Luisa said she would meet me there in an hour. I left through the rear door. As I walked past the porch, the front door opened and I turned away, afraid I'd be called back. It was only Joel. He waved at me and went back inside the house.

I walked very slowly, taking almost fifteen minutes to get to Saint Augustine's Church. If indeed there was someone following me, I wanted this *shadow* to catch up. He had not. At that moment, it didn't matter, for I was content to be in the church, with its lingering scent of beeswax and incense that brought back so many childhood memories.

A few pews away from me, a woman was kneeling, saying the rosary. Unlike Sylvia Castañeda's din in Reyna's ear, I found this woman's continuous recitation in Spanish soothing.

I let myself drift for a while with my eyes closed. The feeling of an almost empty church has always relaxed me. In Oakland sometimes I went to the Chapel of the Chimes or to the adjoining cemetery on a small hill overlooking the bay. Many of the old Oakland families were buried in the cemetery in plots or vaults shaded by pines, oaks and magnolias, but I didn't go there for the view or the history so much as for the solitude it offered.

I opened my eyes again when I heard a creak of hinges on my right-hand side. When I had first walked into the church, I had noticed the door to the rectory was the only way leading to the altar, but it was now hidden from view by the large pedestal and statue of the patron saint. When I looked in the direction of that door, I saw a priest walk in. He genuflected before the altar. Kissing the stole in his hand, he placed it around his neck before walking across the aisle, then into a confessional on my left-hand. A man, who had walked in at the same time as the priest, went into the other cubicle of the confessional.

I liked watching the rituals in the Catholic Church, too. There were even times when I agreed with my grandmother who complained bitterly about the reform of the liturgy. Most of the time, however, I tried to convince her that Latin was a dead language, irrelevant to the lives of millions of Catholics in the world. My argument was of no consequence to her.

In the end, it doesn't matter what language we use, really, for we need rituals and ceremonies to give us a sense of life as something more than routine, more than need, injustice and death. No matter how bedraggled our spirits, I thought, when we walk into a temple, we partake of the divine and we have hope. Luisa said something like that to me once, but she was talking about poetry and its importance in our daily lives. Luisa is a poet, and perhaps for that reason, she has often been able to articulate in a special way what we all feel.

I closed my eyes again, just as the woman saying the rosary made the sign of the cross. After a while she got up and went to light a votive lamp. It was then that I again felt a presence, very close this time. A voice whispered behind me: "Don't look, just listen. I gotta talk to you, but not now. Meet me, tonight."

"Where?" I said, turning my head slightly. I could see only a bare arm and part of the Santos vest, enough to let me know Mando was behind me.

"No, don't turn. *En el patio de la escuela.*"

"Saint Augustine School? The one across the street from this church?" I had passed the school on my way there. "Can my friend Luisa come with me?"

"Yeah, but don't bring that *vato.*" It was obvious Mando had developed an aversion to Joel. I didn't know why, but I wasn't going to question him about it just then.

"What time?" I asked him.

"*A las diez.* There's a hole in the fence next to the parking lot. Go in and wait for me."

Wait, don't go, I wanted to say, but Mando was already leaving. His pants rustled as he moved towards one of the exits on my right side. A few seconds later, up front, the door to the rectory opened again, but no one entered the dimly lit sanctuary.

I could hear unintelligible murmurs coming from the confessional and the creaking of wood when either the priest or the penitent shifted position.

I knelt down, folded my hands, and rested my forehead on them. I threw a furtive glance in the direction of the rectory door that opened onto the altar, and out of the corner of my eye, I caught a shadow moving. It was darker than the other shadows behind the altar and disappeared quickly. For a second I thought I had only imagined it. Then the noise of the rectory door closing again confirmed that someone had indeed been there.

Hoping to have a better view of the entrance to the rectory, I walked towards the confessional, then sat in the pew next to it. If necessary— if little Michael Cisneros' killer was there—I could always go into the confessional and ask for the priest's help. I thought that he'd probably be grateful for the interruption.

I was looking around to see where all the exits were and how long it would take me to reach any one of them, when Kenyon walked in. He didn't notice me at first, but it was obvious he was looking for someone. When he saw me, he looked genuinely surprised.

"So, Gloria Damasco, you're the one Mando has been tracking," Kenyon smiled. "He has been following you and we've been following him."

"Okay. Now do you believe me?" I was upset with Kenyon, although I really didn't know why. "Why didn't you arrest Mando then?"

"Arrest him?" He was surprised. "What for? We want him as a material witness. True, I could pick him up, but I don't think he'd cooperate." Kenyon looked straight at me. "But he'll talk to *you*. He trusts you."

"Maybe." I was lying and Kenyon knew it. I was caught between a relentless urgency to catch little Michael's killer and my desire to protect Mando. The child was dead already, and even though his death filled me with grief, I couldn't forget that Mando was still alive and perhaps in grave danger. The killer might even be stalking Mando at this very moment. I shuddered at the thought.

"If Mando helps you, is there any way you can help him?" I looked Kenyon straight in the eye.

"I'd try." His voice betrayed no hesitation, but no matter how he tried to cover it up, there was doubt in his eyes.

"You know the Santos might kill him for talking to the police." I wasn't saying anything that Kenyon didn't already know but I still had to say it since he was asking me to put Mando's life in his hands.

"Maybe. But whoever killed the boy will also want to get rid of Mando. This killer is the kind of person who can't afford to leave any loose ends. He'll strike again at the slightest suspicion."

"On the other hand, if Mando cooperates with you, the Santos will suspect him from then on," I said.

Kenyon smiled and, to my surprise, he put his hand on mine and squeezed it. "Maybe not. Gang members are picked up for different reasons all the time."

"But they don't go into a court of law and testify against anyone." I shook my head. "Do you really think the Santos wouldn't suspect him after that?" For the first time I asked myself why I had gotten involved in all this.

Luisa always referred to my kind of predicament as one of the gray areas of conscience. "There are no teachers there," she'd say. "You're on your own."

"Well. The D.A. may offer him immunity and even relocation if he describes any gang activity, past, present or future. I would support that." He sighed. "At least he'd be alive. He'd have a fighting chance."

My imagination had taken flight and I saw a fast-forwarded version of Mando's life—a lifetime of *absolutes*: running always, never stopping, never having enough, never being able to see his family. Was that a life worth living? Was his life under the present circumstances worth the risk of death?

"I see. But the D.A. wouldn't offer relocation to Mando if he testified against a child's murderer. Right?" I glared at Kenyon.

"Well ... no. But ... "

I didn't give him a chance to finish. "What about the killer? How does he rate in comparison to the gangs? Does little Michael matter at all in this whole affair?"

"You bet he does. Michael Cisneros has already been to the top brass about it." Kenyon got up and began to pace up and down the aisle, making the penitent in the confessional stick his head out nervously. Kenyon's cheeks were paler than usual, and tiny beads of sweat were forming around his forehead and lips. He finally stopped pacing and stood with his back to me, but I could see him pop something into his mouth. An aspirin, I thought, but the vial he put back in his coat pocket was for prescription drugs. "Well. What is it going to be, Gloria?"

Kenyon was a cop. Even if he was genuinely interested in seeing that no harm came to Mando, he had to bargain on behalf of the establishment. I too had to bargain—on Mando's behalf. It seemed so unfair for Mando and for me, and even for Kenyon, that we should have to make a pact with the devil. In the middle of the house of God no less! That was *our* legal reality: the deal, the only thing we had to show for centuries of institutionalized injustice. But it was that or nothing.

"I'll try to convince him," I said and got up to leave. "You better find out who else was in the rectory while Mando was here."

"Be careful, Gloria," I heard him say, as he moved towards the door to the rectory. But I paid no attention. My soul worried me a great deal more than my body at that moment.

The penitent had left the confessional and was now reaching over the votive candles to light the one farthest from him, stirring the flames. The shadows behind the altar quivered lightly, then resumed their normal flickering, and everything was as before.

SIX

The Dark Gifts

Luisa was sitting on the steps outside Saint Augustine's when I came out, tears running down my cheeks. She immediately asked me to sit down beside her. Being the oldest in a family of three children, I had always had the job of easing things out for my brothers. Now I liked having Luisa look after me like a big sister.

"What were you doing out here?" I asked her when I calmed down.

"I didn't know what else to do. Right after you left Reyna's house, Joel went out to deliver an article. The others left, too. By then, Reyna was looking really tired, so I suggested she take a bath and go to bed." Luisa shrugged her shoulders and laughed. "Her mother is really something, isn't she?"

"I know what you mean. Money, money, money!"

"Anyway," Luisa continued, "I was coming to meet you earlier than we planned, then I saw Kenyon going in," she said. "I figured he wanted to talk to you alone."

"So you've been here all this time?"

"Twenty minutes, more or less. I stopped at a bookstore and got this." She showed me a used edition of *Alice's Adventures in Wonderland*.

"By any chance, did you see anyone come out of the rectory? I think someone was spying on me inside." I relaxed when she shook her head.

"Maybe Kenyon had one of his men tailing you."

Yes, it was possible that one of Kenyon's men had been guarding the entrance to the rectory. Since I had rushed out of the church, Kenyon had not had a chance to clarify that for me.

"What did Kenyon want?" she asked.

I then related my conversation with Mando, and told her about Kenyon's request that I convince Mando that, for immunity and relocation, he tell the police about gang activities and what he knew about the murder.

"Are you going to do it?"

"Do I *really* have a choice?" I shrugged, then asked her if she'd go with me to talk to Mando.

"I wouldn't miss that for the world." Luisa looked at her watch. "When is your meeting with him?"

"Tonight. At ten."

"It's only eight-thirty now. Wanna grab a bite to eat?"

"Sure."

Since her car was parked behind Saint Augustine's church, across from the Elementary School, we turned the corner and walked around to the back of the church.

Across the street, the school occupied about two-thirds of the block. A chain-link fence surrounded the playground, which was opposite the main school building. Ivy and some overgrown bushes gave the school's neighbors some privacy.

From where I stood I couldn't see the parking lot Mando had chosen for our rendezvous. But I remembered that when we attended Mass at Saint Elizabeth's Church in East Oakland, we used to park on the playground at the elementary school across the street. So I walked to the playground to look for markings of car spaces. They were clearly visible on the ground.

"What are we supposed to be doing now? Looking for clues, my dear Miss Marple?" Luisa asked facetiously.

"No. I'm just reconnoitering. We don't want to be fumbling in the dark later, looking for the parking lot and the break in the fence."

We got in the car, and Luisa drove slowly until I spotted the opening in the fence. It was covered somewhat by some overgrowth from the neighboring houses. Then, as we drove past the rectory we saw Kenyon standing by the door talking to Father Mendoza.

Feeling a lot calmer, I was even tempted to tell Luisa about my unusual experiences since Saturday, but on second thought I decided against it. People usually laugh at such things, and I myself had made fun of anything that smacked of psychic phenomena.

Suddenly, Luisa said, "At some point, you're going to have to tell me what's really bothering you."

She must have been reading my mind, I thought, glad she had given me the opportunity to talk about my experiences. "I want to tell you, but I'm not sure even I understand what's been happening." I took a deep breath, primarily to give myself time to decide how to tell her my secret.

Luisa responded with a smile, then advised, "Pretend you're a poet. People are never shocked by anything I say as a poet." She laughed.

"They assume what I say is the product of a weird but creative imagination. Actually, the odder the better."

"I know I'm not going crazy. I feel perfectly sane," I said as I began to tell her about my "flying" experience and the visions triggered by the newspaper clipping.

"It sounds like an out-of-body experience. I think that's what it's called."

"That's how I felt, floating up there and looking down at my own body. I've never had this feeling before. I can only describe it as a ... timeless freedom. A second seems an hour, and an hour is forever." I felt blood rushing to my cheeks and a tingle behind my ears. "Nothing except fear seems to hold you back. Somehow I sensed that, and I was afraid to be afraid because that would put an end to my flight." I paused, then asked Luisa, "Have you ever had an out-of-body experience?"

"No, but once or twice when I've been writing a poem I've felt something similar to what you're describing. Have you told Darío about this?"

"Are you kidding me? He's a medical doctor. He believes only in what is scientifically verifiable. If I told him any of this, he probably would assume I'm on LSD or some other drug. I don't think Darío would understand this at all." I took a deep breath. "I'm not sure that I myself understand or accept what's been happening to me."

Luisa was quiet for a few seconds, then said, "There are things one may not understand, but, still, one accepts them. I don't know where poetry comes from, but I know I'm moved to write poems and I accept that." She paused briefly while she looked for the street sign. Then she went on talking. "There are things that can't be grasped intellectually. Maybe all this seems strange to you because you don't rely much on your intuition and perception of people and things. But I don't think what you've just described is strange at all."

"Without reasoning ... " I started to say, but stopped, put off a bit by Luisa's remarks, even though they weren't intended as any kind of criticism. I hadn't realized until then how touchy I felt whenever a conversation turned to any topic that might put into question a woman's intellectual ability.

"What wins?" Luisa asked facetiously. "Intuition or reason?"

I smiled. "I suppose you're right. Yet what I've experienced is not quite like writing poetry. It's as if someone had suddenly changed all the connections," I said.

"Or as if you stayed on the party line and overheard somebody else's conversation." Luisa smiled at me. "Except this is a far more dangerous situation. I'm sure you're aware that getting involved in this investigation puts you at risk. Even Joel and Reyna are worried about you. He insisted on following you when you left for the church, and I equally insisted that he didn't need to do that." She pulled up in front of the Tapatío restaurant and turned off the motor. "I think Joel smells a good story in all this and wants to stick close to you."

"Maybe that's why Mando doesn't trust Joel," I commented.

"I don't blame Mando. Just look at the way Joel behaved towards him." Luisa puckered her lips, then shook her head. "Joel went from meekness to excessive aggressiveness in a matter of seconds. Anyone can see that he definitely has some problems."

"Maybe it's the influence of his mother-in-law."

"No kidding. I'd go mad with someone like her around me all the time." Luisa put her hands on her head. "Unfortunately Reyna is pretty much like her mother," she continued. "Except she's not quite as greedy. Not yet, anyway."

"What do you mean?"

"Reyna is ambitious and conceited. Manipulative, too. She certainly manipulates Joel."

"Well, you know people spoil beautiful women. Reyna *is* beautiful. She's had two kids, but look at her figure and her skin."

"Joel seems very insecure with Reyna, like he has to keep an eye on her all the time because someone might take her away from him. And she encourages him to think that." Luisa ran her fingers through her hair. "I think he actually has reason to feel threatened ... "

"Why? Is she having an affair?"

"Not exactly." Luisa hesitated for a moment. "I guess I might as well tell you. Reyna's son is not Joel's child. The boy's father is the owner of that butchershop, 'El torito.' A real Don Juan. At the time Reyna got pregnant, he was married, but about two months ago, this Torito's wife finally saw him for what he was and left him."

"And now he's coming after Reyna again?"

"Right. So Reyna has taken advantage of this man's attention to pressure Joel into getting a full-time job. But Joel is an artist and doesn't want to put in the hours required by a full-time job. Who knows? She may be seriously smitten by the Torito owner. He's got the kind of money she wants, and he's opening two more butcher shops soon."

"Poor Joel. I mean that literally. I hate to say it but he's certainly not your run-of-the-mill Latin lover or Prince Charming—and on top of that, he's poor. Why did Reyna marry him in the first place?" I looked at Luisa, who was staring at me with raised eyebrows. "Oh, yeah! You don't have to tell me. Reyna was pregnant and Joel was the answer, right?"

We went into the restaurant, but we didn't eat much. I was beginning to feel exhausted, and Luisa didn't particularly care to stay there. So we decided to go back to the school and park at a vantage point to keep an eye on the playground until it was time to meet Mando. When we got there, we found that the church had been closed right after evening Mass and the street was deserted.

The desolation of the place made me remember how I used to sit in the dark as a child, daring the devil and other creatures of the night to come get me. Nothing compared to that thrill—the rush of fear through my veins at the softest creaking or the dimmest shadow, my heart at full gallop, every hair on my body standing straight up. To cover all bases, every so often I would say a *Hail Mary*. Then, when neither the devil nor any other creature showed up, I'd get an incredible feeling, a mixture of anger and pleasure. Even at that early age I knew that courage was made of those feelings—the "dark gifts" I called them. I felt I might be in need of my dark gifts if things with Mando were to work out.

At 9:50 sharp, Luisa and I got out of the car and made our way as quietly as possible to the playground. We crouched together in the darkest spot we could find, with our backs to one of the neighboring houses. From there we had a clear view of the street and the back of the church to our right. We could also see the school buildings to our left and across from us. I suddenly realized that both Luisa and I were hyperventilating.

I watched the playground. A few minutes later, the shape of a man moved along the wall of the main building. It wasn't Mando. Of that I was sure. I poked Luisa in the ribs with my elbow, took her hand and pointed it in the direction of the shadow. She directed my hand towards the juniper bushes next to Saint Augustine's Rectory.

"One," Luisa whispered in my ear. I felt her quick breathing on my hair. My own heart was threatening to leap out of my mouth with every breath. Suddenly, it dawned on me that the man hiding behind the juniper bushes was probably Matthew Kenyon. He had no doubt seen us poking around the playground, looking for the opening in the fence, and had obviously figured out what we were doing. After that he must have followed us. Damn it! I had been such a fool. What would happen to Mando now? He was walking into a trap and I was being used as bait. I felt the blood rushing to my face, just as I heard Mando's voice say from behind us, "Why did you bring *him*?"

"I didn't," I rasped. I tried to clear my throat without making any noise but couldn't. "Please believe me."

He didn't answer. I panicked and stood up. In a louder voice I said, "Please help us. Tell the police what you know. They will help you in turn. Kenyon promised ... " The rustle of his pants told me he was moving away. "Please." I started towards the opening in the fence. "Mando, please listen to me."

Luisa, who had said nothing, pulled me down. "Mando," I said again, closing my eyes, trying to pick up his presence. Realizing that I had to get us all out of the mess I had created, I began to control my fear, to make my mind take over. Slowly I regained my confidence.

I looked left and right for the two shadows, but couldn't see either one of them. "Did you see where they went?" I asked Luisa.

"See that tree across from the rectory? Someone is there." Her voice was steady, but I felt her hand shaking as she grabbed my wrist. "I don't know where the other one is."

I felt sure that Mando was still around. Scanning the playground, I glimpsed a single shadow moving along the wall of the school building. Then, it disappeared down the pathway, behind the building.

"If you were Kenyon," I asked Luisa, "which spot would you choose? The one on my left or the one on my right?"

"The one on the right," Luisa answered promptly. She had thought about the same possibility.

"I'm going to try to catch up with Mando. You can stay here if you'd rather," I told Luisa, giving her an option, even though I knew what she would do.

"I'm going with you," she answered. "At the count of three."

We were ready to make a run for the opening in the fence when we heard Kenyon's voice coming from our left. "Come on out now." Luisa and I gasped. He came closer and signaled with his flashlight to the man by the tree.

It was a warm evening, but suddenly I was shivering and the muscles around my mouth were jerking uncontrollably. I walked up to Matthew Kenyon and, without the slightest warning, raised my hand and swung it towards his face. If it hadn't been for Luisa holding back my hand, I would have slapped him and, most likely, would have ended up in jail. I glared at him, then walked away, followed by a thoroughly perplexed Luisa.

Perhaps he wasn't any more to blame than I was. But I had trusted him and he had taken advantage of my trust. I sat in the car, deaf to all sound, unable to focus eye or mind on anything except on that horrible certainty: I had betrayed Mando. I would have to find him now, but not by following the glimmer of his presence. I owed him the best of my intuition, my reason and my sweat. Like Mando, I had lost my innocence somewhere between yesterday and tonight. Through him I had rediscovered the dark gift of courage.

SEVEN

The Trap Door

My mother kept telling me that Tania was wet, and as I took off my daughter's wet underwear, I noticed the change in the skin around her thighs. Someone seemed to have cut strips of loose skin, then shaped them into clusters of reddish beads on short strings, three or four strings to a cluster. I couldn't see my mother, but I was able to hear her reproachful voice. "Gloria Inés, you've been so careless. Negligent. I'm taking Tania with me. Now." But I knew my mother couldn't possibly take Tania because I simply wouldn't let her. I took a jar of dark green jelly and began to work on Tania's skin in a gentle kneading motion to smooth it out. Perspiration ran down my forehead, collecting around my eyes. I wiped it off with the back of my index fingers, my eyes half closed. When I opened them again, I suddenly realized that it was Mando's skin I was trying to smooth out.

At that moment, the phone rang, and I heard Kenyon's voice on the line. Hardly any light was coming through the curtains. So I asked him to wait while I turned on the light. It was 5:30 in the morning.

"How soon can you get to the police department?" he asked.

"Why? What's happened?" I was still trying to wipe the dreamweb from my mind and the tears from my eyes.

"I'd rather tell you when you get here." He sounded extremely unsociable.

No doubt he resented my behavior of the night before, but I knew he wouldn't call me at the crack of dawn out of a desire to punish me for it. I agreed to meet him at the station.

When I awoke Luisa to ask her for the keys to her car, she insisted on going along. We hardly talked on the way to the L.A.P.D. There was a remote possibility that Kenyon had caught little Michael's killer. But, without speaking to each other about it, we both sensed that Kenyon wouldn't call at such an ungodly hour unless someone else had died.

53

When we arrived at his office, Kenyon was sitting at his desk and didn't make any attempt to stand up as we entered. The bags under his eyes were quite visible, and the skin on his cheeks and forehead looked paler than usual. With his hand he motioned us to the chairs in front of him.

The instant we sat down he came to the point: "We found Mando dead, stabbed." He held up a knife in a plastic bag, the kind of knife soldiers use in hand-to-hand combat. I would have expected to have seen more blood on it. "No fingerprints, of course," he added.

I got up, but my legs were shaking and I had to sit down again. I heard a hoarse, rhythmic sound. Thinking that Luisa was making the noise, I turned to look at her, but she was sitting quietly, a silent stream running down her cheeks. Then I realized the noise was coming from my own throat and I couldn't make it stop. After a few seconds, it quieted to a wheeze. I held my breath; then, blowing the air gradually out through my nose, I counted from one to eight, as I used to do during swimming lessons at school. As soon as I began to inhale again, my anxiety eased somewhat. Kenyon offered us water in paper cups. Luisa didn't want any, but I took a cup and sipped slowly.

Looking around the office to keep my mind off the knife that had killed Mando, I noticed a photo on the wall. It was of a police awards ceremony. In it, chief of police was giving Kenyon a medal and a plaque. As I fixed my eyes on the photo, a ghost image of the picture began to form and I closed my eyes.

I was moving slowly through a dark place, a warehouse of sorts, hot and misty, as if someone had opened the valves of a steam locomotive. Except for Mando, who was moving away from me, the place was empty. Suddenly, a shadow, with an even darker face, came towards him out of nowhere. Then, I saw a knife in a gloved hand strike straight ahead—a precise incision, through which only a little amount of blood spilled. Mando reached to his chest, keeled over, and laid face down. The dark-faced shadow swiftly moved out of sight. Finally, silence and darkness enveloped the scene.

When I opened my eyes, Kenyon was looking bemusedly at me. He was clearly baffled by my behavior, but no more than I was at this new side of my personality that was making me act so out of character.

"Where was he killed?" I asked without looking at Kenyon. "When?" I met his gaze.

"About three o'clock this morning." He lowered his eyes then looked at me sympathetically. "We found him at the same place where you found the boy."

"He was killed there? Is that what you're saying?" Kenyon was being evasive and I resented his attitude. "Did you call me here to tell me only half the truth?" It was an arrogant thing to say, but I hadn't made peace with him or myself yet for betraying Mando. Somewhere in my subconscious, guilt lay. But I could see in Kenyon's eyes that he shared it too.

"No, he wasn't killed there." He looked at the knife in the plastic bag. "He lost a good deal of body fluid before he died."

"Isn't that what happens when people die? Or are you saying that Mando lost a lot of blood?"

"No, it wasn't blood he lost. The coroner says Mando's skin showed signs of dehydration." Kenyon held the plastic bag up, pointing at the blade and the tip of the knife, then said, "It was quick. In and out in a few seconds. The bleeding was mostly internal." He ennumerated the facts in an almost clinical manner. Then, still in a matter-of-fact tone asked, "Now, why didn't *he* take the knife with him?"

"This killer ... he seems to know what he's doing," I said under my breath. "No messes, no tell-tale signs. Only those he wants us to notice." Rather than attempting to communicate with Kenyon, I was simply thinking aloud, but he heard and looked at me with a half-amused, half-ironic smile.

"We'll catch him." He emphasized the "we" by pointing at me, then at himself.

Even if he felt remorse at abusing my trust the night before, I figured that he could always justify his actions by using his job as an excuse. But I had no way of excusing what I had done—I had no god, no devil to blame. Since I had no way of knowing what he felt, I ignored his remark and continued, "We know that both little Michael and Mando were most likely killed somewhere other than Marigold Street, where we found them." Kenyon nodded; so I went on. "The killer seems to be a man skilled in the use of weapons, with knowledge of the area and the Santos gang's activities. There's also the possibility that he might have planned this a long time ago, and was just waiting for the right moment. And what better opportunity than to have the Cisneros come to town to participate in the march? He couldn't possibly have known that the demonstration would turn into a riot, though. But since the march had been planned in advance, he must have kept abreast of the preparations, and perhaps even had some inside knowledge about the mobilization of police."

"Interesting!" Luisa piped in. I welcomed her interruption.

It's strange how we keep some ideas and feelings from surfacing all

along, then suddenly we say something, even if in a whisper, and the
weight of what we've just expressed drops off our consciousness like a
rock into a quiet pool. In all this time, I hadn't really thought about the
various possibilities. What kind of people would have the inside knowledge required to execute such an elaborate plan so precisely? Someone
who monitored the area, like a postman or a delivery man? But they
wouldn't necessarily have knowledge of weapons or know about the
projected mobilization of police. Could it be that Mando had been trying to protect another member of the Santos? A newspaper would also
have access to the information. So far, I knew of only one newspaperman
covering the Moratorium for the *L.A. Times,* but there were other newspapers. I would have to ask Joel if he knew about other reporters. Since
almost every city cop and L.A. County sheriff deputy met the qualifica-
tions I had just ennumerated, I found myself thinking about what Joel had
said the day before, that the cops were the most logical suspects. And
here I was, spilling my innermost thoughts to a cop. My heart began to
race.

Kenyon's face rested on his folded hands. Both his index fingers
rose up, as if to keep his feelings and thoughts from escaping through
his half-parted lips. Not a trace of irony was evident anywhere in his
face. But he wasn't lost in thought; he had heard every word I'd said.
I just hoped he didn't read minds as well. He'd already betrayed me,
and through me, Mando as well. Yet my instinct told me that Kenyon
could be relied on, that he couldn't possibly have anything to do with the
murders of the child and the young man.

It was time to stop my soliloquy. "Could the killer be a soldier?"
I asked, trying to guide the conversation away from the possibility of
police complicity. The darker face I'd seen in my vision a few minutes
ago appeared to be greasy, like the face of a soldier or a guerrilla fighter
who's trying to camouflage his presence. "That *is* a trench knife, isn't
it?"

Kenyon looked at me, then at the knife. He smiled. "Very impressive,
Gloria. Very impressive."

Smiling and blushing at the same time, I said, "I've seen enough
war movies to recognize one of those. So, do you think he might be a
soldier?"

"It's possible." He nodded. "He might not be a soldier any more, but
this man, the one who killed Mando, probably had some kind of military
training."

"Are you saying that the person who killed Mando might not be the
same one who killed little Michael?" I asked. Knowing that Kenyon

could end our conversation at any time, I added, "It would make sense. After all, Mando was the only one who saw the killer. But ... " I realized that Kenyon and I kept running against the same obstacle. "Although we don't know why, we do know that little Michael was drugged and strangled. Mando, on the other hand, died because he could identify the child's murderer, but he was killed in such a different way."

Kenyon looked up. "Unless ... "

Luisa rapped on my arm. "Unless what?" she said irritably. "Unless there are ... two killers?" Unable to control her excitement, she gasped, then asked again, "You really think that there are two murderers?"

"There may be more than one arm, but there's a likelihood that a single master mind planned all this," Kenyon explained.

"A *conspiracy*?" Luisa's eyes opened wide.

"I'm not so sure it's a conspiracy," I said. "But if there are two killers, then ... "

I had no intention of placing us in jeopardy, so I stopped midway through my thought. Kenyon would have to tell us his reason for asking us to come to his office. He was an intelligent man and a good cop. Surely he didn't need our help in solving these two murders. So, more than likely, he needed some information he thought or hoped we had.

Feeling confident that I was right, I said, "I think it's time you tell us why you brought us here at the crack of dawn. You could have told me about Mando's death on the phone. And you didn't bring us all the way down here just to help you brainstorm."

He gave me a quick glance. Then, opening his notebook, he told us, "I'd like you to tell me what Mando said to you, word by word."

"You mean, last night?" Luisa asked, seeking clarification about the information he wanted.

"And at any other time. Go back to Saturday, to the first time Mando talked to you." He looked hard at Luisa and at me. "Don't think too much, Gloria. Just talk. If you forget something," he told me, "she can fill in the gaps." He nodded towards Luisa.

"Luisa, why don't you tell him about what happened on Saturday?" I begged.

For the next ten minutes, Luisa talked about everything she remembered, from the moment we first saw little Michael lying on the sidewalk until the time Joel and I returned from the Galeanos' house. Then, I related in detail my conversation with the Galeanos, and how Joel had cautioned me against calling the cops. I also described my experience with the police department when I called to report the death.

I watched for Kenyon's reaction to Joel's warning about the police, but he showed no sign of either surprise or anger. With his head lowered, he listened attentively to everything, writing things down as we talked. "You said Galeano volunteered to go with you to take photographs. Where are they?"

"I don't know. I don't think Joel has developed the film yet, or he would have shown them to us yesterday. We were at his house."

"Did you go to his house before or after meeting with Mando yesterday?"

"Before."

He wrote down question and answer, and rapped lightly with his pencil on the notebook.

"Did you know you'd run into Mando at Saint Augustine's?"

"I guess I did figure he'd be there. I'd had this—this feeling that he was following me."

"That *somebody* was following you or that *he* in particular was following you?" He looked up.

"I felt that he, Mando, was following me." Blood rushed to my cheeks, making my face warm all over. "Don't ask me how I knew. I just knew."

"Did anyone else know he was following you? Did you tell anybody besides 'Dr. Watson' here?" Smiling, he pointed at Luisa with the pencil.

"I don't think anyone else knew about it," I reassured Kenyon. Holding back a smile, I added. "Not even Dr. Watson here knew about Mando following me."

Kenyon grinned at Luisa and she grinned back. The poet and the homicide detective. A fantasy began to take shape in my imagination, but I quickly dismissed it. Coming back from my brief reverie, I caught sight of Luisa looking amusedly at me, as if she could read what I had been thinking. But perhaps it was simply the way good friends who have known each other for a long time learn to read each other gestures and attitudes.

Reflecting on my friendship with Luisa made me realize I didn't know anything about Mando. Did he have any brothers or sisters? Did anyone know Mando well? Did he confide in anyone? Had he wanted me to be his friend? My thoughts and feelings were quickly tying themselves into nooses around my conscience, and I began to feel awful.

Kenyon cleared his throat and I was grateful for the interruption. "So, Gloria, tell me about Sunday."

I talked about our conversation with Otilia regarding Lillian, the gathering at the Galeanos' house, my meeting with Mando and my suspicion that someone had been watching me from the rectory.

"We couldn't tell if anyone else was there," he pointed out. Father Mendoza was the only priest at the church at the time, and as you said, he was in the confessional." He shook his head. "The Padre had forgotten to lock the outside door to the rectory before he went to hear confessions. So anyone, maybe even one of the neighborhood kids, could have walked in unnoticed." He fell silent for awhile.

I doubted that Kenyon really believed one of the kids had walked into the rectory, but he had to explore every possibility before making a move. Did he, like Darío, play chess? I wondered. Darío was one of the most gentle men I had ever known, but he became Count Dracula when he was let loose on a chessboard. I was no match for him. My husband and Kenyon would probably play well together.

Kenyon then asked Luisa to tell him what had happened at the Galeanos' house after I had gone to the church. Luisa had very little to report since Joel had left shortly after I did, followed by some of his guests.

"So most people left right after Gloria went to church?" he clarified, and Luisa agreed. He looked at a paper on his desk. "Did Joel leave with the others or before them? Did he have his camera with him when he left the house?"

"He got ready to leave before the others, but in the end almost everyone walked out at the same time. And yes, he had his camera with him." Luisa turned towards me. Kenyon ignored the look that passed between Luisa and me. I was getting ready to ask him what all this was about, but he turned to me and said, "Now tell me about your night meeting with Mando."

Frankly, I didn't understand his reason for asking us all those questions. "You were there," I said angrily. "You tell us."

Although I respected Kenyon's intelligence, and my intuition told me he wouldn't turn on us, Luisa and I could not afford not to be on the defensive. For the second time in two days, I wondered why I'd gotten involved in this investigation. Yet, almost immediately, I answered my own question, as I remembered Mando looking at little Michael's body before handing me the clipping. Mando's and the boy's murders were more real than ever, and the memory brought back to me the urgency of making sense of everything that had happened since Saturday. It was too late now to start questioning my involvement.

"What do you want to know?"

"Just tell me what he said to you," Kenyon requested.

"He asked me why I'd brought you. I don't know how he knew it was you. He had this ... sixth sense about cops."

"Did he mention me by name?" Kenyon inquired, making me wonder if they actually knew each other.

Mando hadn't mentioned Kenyon's name or any other name, I told him. Then I inquired, "Am I to assume that you and Mando knew each other personally?"

He shook his head and tapped on his lips with his index finger. "Could Mando have meant somebody else, and you simply *assumed* he was referring to me after you saw me there? Could he have been talking about Joel or about someone else?"

"Joel?" Luisa was almost shouting. "What are you saying—that Joel has something to do with the murders? C'mon!"

Kenyon remained impassive. "My partner, Jim McGuire, and I spotted Galeano on several occasions while we were tailing Mando."

"A coincidence," Luisa rebutted. "That's all."

"Possibly. But my partner saw Galeano getting into his car last night, after Mando took off." He raised his eyebrows. "My partner didn't see Mando, but we know Galeano was definitely at that school last night. I didn't see Mando either, but I'll take your word for it that he was there."

"But why?" Luisa insisted. "What on earth could possibly make Joel want to kill Mando?" She wiped some invisible sweat from her forehead. "It just doesn't make sense."

"Possibly revenge," Kenyon said, but his eyes revealed a great deal of uncertainty. "My partner told me that a couple of years ago, one of Galeano's Marine buddies—a Viet Nam veteran like Galeano—was assaulted and ended up in the hospital in critical condition," he paused. "I vaguely remember the case. We know his buddy was visiting East L.A. and we also know Galeano was not with him that day. Galeano insisted it was one of the Santos who had jumped his buddy, even though the victim's description of the assailant didn't match the Santos attire. Since then, Galeano has been on a crusade against the gangs. Gangs in general and the Santos in particular are the targets of his anger."

"Do you yourself believe that gangs are that bad?" Luisa asked him.

"It doesn't matter what I believe, does it?"

I had begun to notice that, when asked for his personal opinion, Kenyon always answered a question with a question. I suspected that half of those times his opinion didn't quite match departmental policies or practices.

After responding to Luisa's question, Kenyon looked at me. I didn't say anything, even though I was thinking that Mando hadn't trusted Joel from the beginning. I could almost hear Mando's voice as clearly as I had when he stood right next to me at the church. "Don't bring that other *vato*," he had said.

In an effort to figure out if Kenyon was right in suspecting Joel, I began to piece together what I knew about him. Joel was left-handed. He had been a Marine in Viet Nam. He was now a reporter and a photographer. He was familiar with the *barrio*, and he had been involved in the preparations for the march. Finally, he had a grudge against the Santos. I wasn't sure how his present difficulties at home with Reyna and with her mother fit into the overall picture, but I sensed that something was terribly wrong there.

I saw what Kenyon was driving at as clearly as the sunlight now streaming through the open window of his office. The logic behind his suspicion sent my heart on a wild sprint. Trying to dispel the possibility that Joel had killed Mando, I shook my head, but deep inside I shared Kenyon's doubts. I found myself following Kenyon's every move in my mind in a kind of frantic match, and I envied his detachment and objectivity. For Kenyon, this was a puzzle or a game of deduction and strategy. He took his personal and moral concerns for granted, for in the solution of a crime, justice was somehow served and goodness always prevailed. But goodness, like justice, was only a relative notion, depending on who interpreted or administered it. This much, if nothing else, I had already learned in my twenty-three years.

Feeling confused about what path to follow, I began to wonder if I shouldn't draw the line right there, and refuse to be a part of the investigation. But my life had already become intertwined with the deaths of Michael David and Mando, and with the lives of many others who were now directly or indirectly affected by their deaths. Now Reyna and her children were added to that list.

Nonetheless, telling myself that the evidence against Joel was all circumstantial, pure conjecture, I got up to leave. I thought of asking Kenyon to let me see Mando's body but decided against it. Not seeing him dead would at least temporarily allow me to keep him alive in my mind.

Leaving the door open for Luisa, I walked out of Kenyon's office. I was already half way down the hall when I realized she wasn't behind me, so I waited a few minutes for her to catch up.

"Hey, Gloria. Kenyon is really worried about us. Especially about you. I'm worried about you too, you know." Luisa squeezed my arm. "Maybe you should go back to Oakland. Today. Now. Immediately. Kenyon won't try to stop you." Knowing only too well that Luisa and I were both in danger, I didn't pretend that we shouldn't be concerned. Little Michael's killer wouldn't know that Mando hadn't had time to give us any details about him. Having to look over my shoulder forever certainly wasn't my idea of living, so I knew that in spite of my fear I would not rest until I found out who had killed little Michael and Mando, and the reason behind their death. Could I do it alone or would I need the aid of someone like Kenyon? That was the question I had to answer before I could decide what to do next.

I already knew that something in my psychological make-up had changed. This was the third and darkest of all of the dark gifts. Surely it wasn't much of a gift, I realized. What good were visions if there was no way to decode them? If their effectiveness as a tool to apprehend the murderer was nil?

Luisa interrupted my thoughts. "I don't know what you're going to do, Gloria," she said. "But it might be a good idea to talk to a lawyer before you do anything. I didn't tell you this before because I didn't think it was important, but Frank Olivar wants to talk to you about little Michael's murder."

"Who's Frank Olivar?"

"He's a reporter for the newspaper *La Causa Chicana*, and a friend of Zeta Acosta, the lawyer." Luisa explained. "Both of them were at Joel's house yesterday."

"I didn't meet either one of them. What about Olivar?"

"Frank Olivar and Zeta Acosta thought at first that the police might have had something to do with little Michael's death. I told them what we saw when we found the body." Suddenly, Luisa slowed down and took a long breath, making me realize how tired and frightened she too had been. I put my arm around her shoulder to show her my support and concern. After awhile, she began to relax.

"So, do Olivar and Zeta Acosta think that the police are involved in the murders or don't they?" I asked Luisa.

"They're not really sure. I mean, little Michael was drugged and then strangled, and he had that—that *caca* in his mouth. That's not their idea of how the cops would operate. In their way of looking at things, the cops would have made it look like an accident. No muss, no fuss." Luisa shrugged her shoulders. "I just thought Zeta Acosta might be able to give you some legal advice, maybe tell you what you can do about all this."

"I'll call him," I said, mainly to reassure her. I had come into this case through a trapdoor of the psyche, and it might take me years to find my way out of that netherworld to the truth. Knowing that I would not be able to uncover the answer without Kenyon's help, and that Luisa's and my own safety depended on my actions, I decided to go back to Kenyon's office and ask him what he intended to do about Joel.

I asked Luisa to wait for me in the car while I talked to Kenyon. He seemed not to have moved a muscle since we left him. He was looking straight at the door, his chin still resting on his folded hands. But I knew he had been expecting me.

"Why not just pick up Joel for questioning?" I asked.

"There isn't enough solid evidence to warrant bringing him in. He would be out again in a few hours. If he's part of the conspiracy and we alert him, the child's murderer will be on his guard as well. Then we may never catch him. But if someone close to Galeano, someone he might not suspect, lures him into a trap, we might be able to catch two birds ... "

Kenyon's plan made sense, even if I still refused to believe Joel was guilty.

"And that someone is me, right?" I exclaimed.

"If you agree, I'll pick you up at your friend's house in two hours." He looked at his watch. "That is, at 10:30." He threw a quick glance at me. "But you'll have to be absolutely sure you want to do this."

"Yes," I answered. Black Queen to White King's Bishop three, I thought, then added, "But you must promise me that you'll give Joel the benefit of the doubt: innocent until proven guilty."

I suspected that Kenyon would lie and agree to anything I asked, and that I wouldn't be able to ascertain if he was telling the truth or not. But what if Kenyon was right and Joel had killed Mando? Was it wise for me to ignore that possibility? I felt I had no choice but to put myself under Kenyon's care. If he was on the right track, my life also depended on how skillfully and dispassionately I could play the game. And I had no intention of losing this match.

EIGHT

Mires and Butterflies

Luisa rushed out to work, but not before begging me again to consider carefully the personal and political consequences of what I was about to do. Sipping my coffee, I thought about them while I watched a late butterfly slowly crawl out of its cocoon, hidden under the ravaged leaf of a potted nasturtium on the kitchen window.

Moved by mere instinct, a voracious green caterpillar had recently foraged the leaves on their twisted slender limbs, unaware of the life of ephemeral beauty it was to lead after its chrysalis stage. And now, I thought, oblivious to its earthbound instincts as a caterpillar, the butterfly was emerging, ready to suck the nectar of flowers and to keep company with the wind.

Whereas my grandmother, Mami Julia, wouldn't conceive of killing a butterfly, I remembered she hadn't had any qualms about squashing the caterpillar to save her plants. "It looks like a green worm to me," she would say when I pointed out that killing a caterpillar was the same thing as exterminating a butterfly.

How simple decisions were for my grandmother, I mused, how black or white the moral question in them. In comparison, the dilemma in which I found myself had no easy solutions.

In the summer of 1970 everything anyone of us did had to be considered according to its political impact on the Chicano community. So Luisa and I supported the unwritten rule that forbade Chicanos to go public on any issues that could be used to justify discrimination against us.

In some ways, I realized, our movement for racial equality and self-determination was no different from others like it in other parts of the world. But we were a people within a nation. Our behavior was constantly under scrutiny, our culture relentlessly under siege.

Caught between political ideologies whose ends and means were diametrically opposed, like most people of our generation, Luisa and I treaded on a quagmire of the conscience. At every step, the pros and cons of peaceful or armed struggle weighed heavily upon us. Without supporting the radical notion that every Chicano in jail was a "political prisoner," we accepted as our right and responsibility the function of making sure that justice was dealt equally to everyone.

For years, I'd walked around with unresolved anger delicately balanced against the hope in my heart that one day our social and political condition would improve for us. But when I found little Michael's body during the most violent confrontation I had ever had to face, the balance was upset, the fragile order broken.

Obeying the outrage, I felt there was no other course of action but to serve as bait to lure Joel out in the open. Trying to rationalize my decision, I told myself that Joel's innocence could be proven in this way, too. Kenyon had only circumstancial evidence in support of his accusation. It was true that Joel was a trained soldier who knew the *barrio* and the gang's moves well. But he had no strong apparent motive for murder. Would Joel have killed Mando just because his war buddy had been assaulted by a gang member? On the other hand, why would he, who seemed so dedicated to the movement, agree to such deplorable complicity? Had he killed anyone else in cold blood? If Kenyon's suspicions were correct, what would Joel have been promised to have him agree to such heineous acts? And what about the person who might have offered such inducement? Who was he? What moved him? How had they met? If Joel's motive had been money, which given his precarious finances was always a strong incentive, then the person who wanted little Michael dead must have access to greater resources than most of us. Still, I asked myself, why would anyone want to kill Michael David Cisneros?

Partly, I realized, I was willing to go along with Kenyon's plan because of my incessant desire to learn the answers to those questions. Since I had no resources available to me, no skills or back-up to find the answers on my own, I had to go along with his plan. If I tried to probe, and if Joel was indeed Mando's murderer and he suspected what I was doing, he would most certainly want to eliminate me—and Luisa, too! If I was wrong about him, I would be politically shamed and lose the trust of many people. What would be worse, to live with shame or to die with my political reputation unblemished? I couldn't help laughing at the absurdity of my question.

"Kenyon can't force me to do anything I don't want to. And I can always change my mind at the last minute," I said aloud. Immediately I felt better but thinking about Kenyon triggered a number of other questions concerning his behavior. Why had he let me, an outsider, become involved? Was he acting on his own, out of rage perhaps? How was he planning to ensure my safety? What would become of Tania if anything happened to me?

And Darío? When he'd shown interest in me, five years before, most of his friends had advised him to stay away from me. I was pleasant to look at but not pretty; and I was too young, too intense, too intelligent and too independent. All capital sins. Chicano nationalism and feminism didn't walk hand in hand before or during the summer of 1970. But Darío didn't listen to any of the well-wishers back in 1965. In time, almost all of them learned to accept me.

What would my husband think of all this? Perhaps this time he wouldn't approve. Although anxiety was building in me, making me want to phone Darío in Oakland or to seek Zeta Acosta's advice, I resisted, willing to face the shame if it came to that. Until then, I had no intention of letting anyone know what I was about to do. Instead of calling Oakland, I reached for the phone book and looked up Otilia Juárez's phone number. Fortunately, she was listed, and I dialed her number.

She answered promptly. "Ah, Gloria. I'm so glad you called. I was about to telephone Detective Kenyon to get your phone number. How are you?"

"I'm all right. How's everybody there?" I was eager to find out why she wanted to call me, but I also wanted to know how Lillian and Michael were doing.

"A little better today. We were having coffee this morning when Barbara, an old friend of Lilly's, came by. I don't know what they talked about, but Lilly cried for a long time. Michael and I were so relieved to see Lilly finally give in to her feelings. We were very grateful to Barbara for that."

"That's a good sign," I said, swallowing hard to undo the knot beginning to form in my throat. "And how is Michael doing?"

"I've been worried sick about him, too. He pretends, for our benefit, I'm sure. But last night, he was out in the yard for a long time, and his eyes were red when he came back in."

"It's always best to express one's feelings. I'm so glad he has you, too, especially with his parents dead and his brother gone for the time being."

"I care a great deal for Michael. But I really wish Paul were here so he could talk to the police and take some of the load off Michael's shoulders."

"Will he be coming back soon?"

"He'll be arriving in San Francisco tomorrow evening. He was on holiday somewhere in Southern Germany—Bavaria, I think—before coming back to the States. His business associates in Germany were not able to get in touch with him until yesterday. But he'll be in Oakland in time for the funeral on Thursday."

"Does that mean you are all going back to the Bay Area soon?"

"Yes. We're leaving on Wednesday. My little Michael is now at the mortuary being prepared for viewing. An evening Mass will be said for him tonight. We've invited only relatives and some close friends. Not many of our relatives will be able to attend the funeral in Oakland, you know. I'd like for you and Luisa to be with us tonight if you can. We're all very grateful to you. Both of you have been kind and thoughtful with us and so helpful in dealing with the police."

"We'd like very much to pay our respect. Where will the Mass be?"

"It's at six, at Saint Augustine's Church. We'll see you then."

Otilia hung up before I could ask her anything else, but she had unknowingly given me another reason to help Kenyon. After calling Luisa to confirm that she too would be able to attend the service, I realized that my conception of time had changed, and that now, I measured its passing by the number of hours or minutes or seconds to the next twist or turn in this bizarre case. In half an hour Kenyon would pick me up and brief me on his entrapment plan, but the evening church service was eight hours away, and I shuddered to think that I might not make it to Saint Augustine's. Thinking of Lillian's grief, I closed my eyes. Her words *"What have I done ... This is my pool of tears ... "* Rippled softly on the quiet of my mind. Then they drowned in a soulful melody I'd heard before but couldn't quite identify at the moment. Lillian's profile flashed through my mind, then the song stopped. When I opened my eyes, my hands were trembling.

NINE

Mires and Mirrors

After showering and dressing, I checked my face in the mirror and chose the right eyeshadow to go with my blue blouse. Dead but presentable, I thought, laughing at my own incongruity when I heard the doorbell. Matthew Kenyon and a policewoman in uniform smiled at me as I peered through the narrow opening allowed by the safety chain.

The policewoman, Anne Louise Morgan according to her name tag, took out a small tape recorder, a microphone, and some wires to connect one to the other.

"Is this the best you can do for a Chicana?" I knew I had asked a rhetorical question, a grounding to avoid overloading the panic circuits in my mind.

"State of the art," said Kenyon, trying to be humorous. "Just for Chicano women."

"I think I better start your education right now. You have to say Chicanas with an "a" when you talk about us women. Got it?"

He nodded, carried a chair from the kitchen and sat astride it. Officer Morgan replaced the batteries in the small recorder, ejected the tape and loaded it again, then tested the recording level. She seemed quite handy with the gadgets. Kenyon watched her go through her technical checklist, with a strange look in his eyes. Knowing that she was being watched, every so often she looked at him out of the corner of her eye. Once, perhaps long ago, there had been some intimate moments shared, or at least the desire for intimacy between them.

"Can I ask you something personal?" My question startled him, and I laughed. "Why are you letting me do this? I don't know much about who's who in the L.A.P.D., but are you sure you won't be getting me in trouble?"

"I'm in worse trouble if I don't do this." He threw a quick glance at Officer Morgan and she smiled. "Don't worry. I'll definitely protect you."

"Don't start talking to me in riddles," I said, then added, "What does your partner think about all this? Should I pay a visit to your local legal aid office?"

He didn't find my comment amusing, even though I had smiled as I said it. "Let's just say that I'm beyond punishment. That means anything goes," he said in all seriousness.

Trying to make sense of what he said seemed useless, for he obviously didn't want to discuss whether he had the authority or not to get me involved in his investigation. I began to feel uneasy, but I reminded myself that I could change my mind at any time.

Officer Morgan asked me to follow her into the bedroom and to show her my other clothes. The blue blouse had to go, she told me; it was too tight around my waist. The small tape recorder was going to be taped on my back while the microphone would be put below my bra. She chose instead a long-sleeved lavender blouse and a light loose vest that could be worn over my jeans. The outfit easily camouflaged the presence of the recorder and microphone. This Monday was another hot day in L.A., and I could already see myself perspiring. Think cool I told myself, but my hands were already sweaty, so I wiped them on my blouse.

Officer Morgan motioned me to sit on the bed beside her. "Listen, you don't have to do this if you don't want to." She patted my hand.

"It's so tough," I said. "One minute I'm ready to go and the next ... I want to do the right thing, but I feel I'm being used." I stood up and leaned on the dresser, facing her. "Look, Officer Morgan. You just saw what happened. He avoided answering my questions ... "

"Call me Anne, please. I know you want reassurance." She smiled, but her eyes were sad. "All I can tell you is that he's a good cop. And by that I mean he's compassionate, fair-minded, honest and a damned good homicide investigator. One of the best. He wouldn't be asking you to do this if he weren't pretty sure Galeano is implicated."

After I agreed to let her continue taping the equipment on me, she secured the small recorder onto the left side of my lower back in such a way that I could manipulate the buttons. Record and play modes were together in a single button, and that made things easier. Coiling the slim cables, she taped them under my bra, placing the small microphone under my breast so that it would pick up any sound, but not be easily noticed.

"Why is Kenyon ... ?" Speaking my mind was something I liked in myself, but the events of the last two days had made me cautious almost to the point of paranoia.

"Why is he going about it this way?" Anne volunteered, "I shouldn't be telling you this, but this might be his last case. And it's proving to be the toughest."

"Is he going to retire soon? He doesn't seem that old." Suddenly, I recalled the vial with the prescription pills he was taking. "Is he ill?" I asked hesitantly.

Anne didn't say a word, but her face told me what I needed to know.

"He's dying," I whispered. "That explains ... "

Things began to fall into place, as a number of coincidences now became a series of related events with all of us as protagonists. Perhaps Luisa was right. Fate was the great equalizer in this situation. "Okay," I said, pointing to the equipment on the bed. "Why don't we finish getting this wire on me?"

In addition to the recorder, she also had a small device that looked a great deal like the beeper Darío had to wear while on call outside the hospital. It was a transmitter, Anne explained. The red button had to be pressed twice for a warning, once for requesting immediate assistance. My life depended on this red button. After running a couple of tests, I tucked the transmitter into the pocket of my jeans.

Anne and I went back into the living room. Since we hadn't heard even a sigh out of him for half an hour, I thought Kenyon had surely fallen asleep or that he had left. But he was still there, sitting astride the chair. His eyes showed such anguish that I found myself overwhelmed by a sudden rush of tenderness towards him.

"For whatever it's worth," I said, "I'm sorry about last night." The words echoed against a wall of my memory. Last night suddenly seemed like such a long time ago.

"I'm sorry about Mando, too." He put his hand on my shoulder. After wishing me good luck, Anne left and Kenyon went with her to her car. I then got my keyring, a ten-dollar bill and my driver's license and put them into the left pocket of my vest. Before walking out, I checked myself in the mirror. Except for some outward changes, I was still the green caterpillar I'd always been, stepping onto the mire with clumsy, uncertain feet.

TEN

High Noon in Hell

Kenyon drove down Whittier Boulevard towards town. Cruising down the boulevard on that last morning of August, one could hardly believe that only two days before, violence had prevailed. Except for a few boarded-up store windows, everything seemed back to normal. For the first time, I realized how enduring the human spirit is, but couldn't help wondering if at times this very quality prevented us from eradicating injustice more quickly.

About a mile down the boulevard, Kenyon turned right. He drove under the freeway, then down a long unpaved road where there were a couple of condemned buildings. One of them was a warehouse of sorts that showed the signs of prolonged neglect. Most of its windows were shattered; dead ivy and graffiti covered its walls.

As we got closer to the gloomy structures, I began to feel anxious. A series of clashing emotions seemed to be trying to resolve their contradictions inside my ears, making me feel lightheaded. "They were killed here—Mando and little Michael, weren't they?"

"I think so. It's quite isolated here, but very close to Marigold Street, as you can see." Kenyon got out of the car.

The desire to make sense of things made me follow him without hesitation. The recorder pressed against my back, making me straighten up.

"Mando's murderer must have known the Santos come here every so often. This is one of their hangouts," Kenyon explained.

"How do you know the Santos use this as a meeting place?"

"McGuire asked one of his pals in the Gangs Activities Section, who knows all about the gangs in East L.A. It seems the Santos meet here, all right."

The smell of excrement assaulted my nostrils and I stopped listening to Kenyon. After looking around, unable to see anything that might cause

71

the foul smell, I thought that it might be rising up from my memory.

"What about the signs of dehydration in Mando's body? This looks like a warehouse not a steam bath, and if he was killed here ... "

"Come inside and you'll see." Kenyon kicked the door open. "The Preston Family of Pasadena owns the property, but they haven't used it in years. They'll probably wind up selling it. Old man Preston was our local variety of genius, always inventing or adapting this or that. He had a coal furnace built to heat water and a small turbine, which worked on the same principle as the steam engine of a train." Kenyon pointed at a place next to the door and then at the ceiling. "See the pipeline? It carried the steam into the greenhouse. Old man Preston loved to grow exotic tropical plants, and he needed the steam to recreate the natural conditions they grow in."

"It sounds a bit eccentric to me. Couldn't he just have used a vaporizer?"

Kenyon chuckled at my ridiculous comment. He walked over to the wall and inspected the pipe by the door. "It looks like someone's been keeping up the plumbing. Pretty good condition. Probably the Santos. I'll take a look at the turbine."

We walked through to the other end of the warehouse. A half-hidden door opened into a large greenhouse. It was made of wood, rubber, tile, iron and glass. Fragile looking but really quite strong, the door was re-enforced on both sides with strips of steel over a rubber lining. The rubber was scratched and torn around the knob, inside as well as outside, probably from the use of a padlock to keep it locked. "Actually," I said, looking around the room, "a vaporizer would be quite useful in a room this big." Another stupid comment, I realized.

"You're right," Kenyon said. "The steam engine was actually something like a vaporizer but bigger and more complex."

It was time to change the subject, so I commented, "You seem to know a lot about this greenhouse."

Kenyon's face lit up. "I like horticulture. It's my hobby. Old man Preston's orchids were famous all over California, especially his epiphytic orchids."

"His epi-what orchids?"

"Orchids that grow on trees in the tropical rain forests." He smiled when I raised my eyebrows, impressed with his lesson in botany. "I read the two books he wrote on the cultivation of rare tropical plants," Kenyon continued. "He hated the term 'exotic'. Everything was exotic in this world, he used to say; not even two plants of the same genus and species were really alike. It all depended on the point of view. Anyway, I knew about this greenhouse from its description in one of Preston's books."

Kenyon looked quite animated, some color even showing in his usually pale complexion. Carrying a long stick he found lying around, he walked into the greenhouse.

"And it occurred to you that the killer knew about the Santos' meetings here and about the little greenhouse." I looked at the tile-covered walls and the small windows. Some of the window panes seemed to be cracked, but I couldn't tell if they actually had any holes in them. "But some of the glass seems broken. Wouldn't the steam escape? If Mando was killed here, how could he then show signs of dehydration?"

"Look again." Kenyon was pointing at the upper two windows. "They're double-paned windows. Even if one breaks, the second one keeps the steam from escaping." He pointed at a frame with the stick. "And rubber was used to make the windows airtight. This weather stripping looks pretty new to me. Someone went to the trouble of replacing the old strips for a reason."

"But why? Why would little Michael's killer go to all this trouble to silence Mando? Why not just kill him and be done with it? And if your calculations are right, why did this person ask Joel to do it?"

"This is someone who is extremely cruel and who takes pride in devising and executing a plan to perfection. He's a strategist, you can be sure of that; and he has a mission. However personal his reason for killing the little boy—and I doubt very much that it is personal—he couldn't be bothered with Mando. He simply arranged for help with that one. He's the boss and he's showing off. He's daring us to catch him."

I assumed his use of the plural pronoun meant the police department, and not Kenyon and me. We had joined forces in the midst of strife. My reasons for agreeing to help Kenyon were obvious to him, but his were still not clear to me. If, as I suspected, he was a man who was running out of time, to ask him for his reasons would be a total disregard for his privacy. During the last two and a half days I had resented Matthew Kenyon, then admired him. I had confided in him only to distrust him later. Now I was beginning to trust him again. I realized at that moment that I also liked him, and that in time I would even miss him. His presence was comforting, and his objective view of things was helping me keep anxiety and grief at bay for a while longer.

The greenhouse was empty of tools, rocks, plants and even pots. The cement floor had recently been painted—most likely by the Santos, as Kenyon had pointed out. It actually made a good steam room. The floor was a bit slanted around the center to facilitate drainage. Beside the vent where the steam came into the greenhouse, the crumbling shells of two trees stood next to a low cement planter. I sat on the edge while Kenyon went down below to check the turbine. The cement seemed unusually warm, and I got up almost immediately, then sat down again. Since the planter was the only place where anyone could sit, Mando must have been sitting on that same spot the night before.

Ever since Saturday, my eyes had been bothering me. I closed them to relieve the irritation and enjoyed the quiet and the cool breeze blowing in through the open door, directly across from the main door of the warehouse. Mando was standing in the center of my mind. He was looking up at something, then down. The steam was coming in incessantly, but he wasn't afraid. Then he began trying to find a way out, to knock the door down. An impossible task. He waited for the killer to come back; he would take his chances with him. But after half an hour, when no one had shown up, the wild beating of his heart told him he was in trouble. Then came the claustrophobia, the burning sensation on his skin when the heat increased. He began licking his own sweat, but he couldn't replace the liquid fast enough. He felt panic taking hold of him, then began to surrender to an overwhelming desire to sleep. His eyes had begun to close when the door opened. Drained of his energy, perhaps even of the desire to live, Mando walked out of that greenhouse exactly at the moment the killer had planned.

Gasping for breath, I opened my eyes. I'd been his last hope, his only chance to have the killer pay for his crime, and I'd failed him. He faced the blade and maybe even welcomed it as the only possible escape. Trying to contain my tears, I started to hiccup. I thought again about Joel's motives. All the questions I carried in my head began floating around like a swarm of mosquitoes.

"I can't believe that Joel Galeano could be that cold-blooded or clever," I said to Kenyon when he joined me again. "It just doesn't make sense. Why would he do something so horrible?" I held my breath as long as I could to stop the spasms in my throat, but they continued.

Kenyon rapped on his lips with his left index finger. I was learning to interpret his body language; this particular gesture meant that he was debating whether he should make me privy to his theory.

"Have you ever read his articles?" he asked me after a long silence. I shook my head, so Kenyon explained further, "He's very dedicated, almost to the point of obsession to that *la causa* of yours. I personally think Galeano is very disturbed. He firmly believes that the gangs are one of the main reasons this society disapproves of Mexicans, and that your people must find a way to get rid of them. In contrast, he thinks that, in the end, people like Rubén Salazar are the ones who will redeem your community."

"Redeem! What's there to redeem? Is that what he said or is it your own interpretation of it?" The sound of my voice rose at least two decibels.

"He used that word a couple of times in that context, and I interpreted it to mean what I just said. I'm not wrong, Gloria. And I'm not against Chicanos getting what's due you." He sat down on the planter next to me. "I've been a homicide cop a long time, maybe too long. You develop an instinct for this kind of thing. It's nothing magic; you just let the evidence speak to you. Your mind does the rest." He headed towards the door of the warehouse. I stayed where I was.

I really didn't know Joel well. Luisa had moved to Los Angeles only a couple of months before and she'd only known the Galeanos since June. But, judging from the conversation we'd had at the restaurant the night before, Reyna had told Luisa a lot about herself.

Pareja dispareja—an odd couple, I remember thinking when I met them. Reyna was quite beautiful. She showed very good taste in the choices she made for herself and her house. With only a few touches here and there, she had made the place look very attractive. But Joel wasn't at all handsome or even attractive. On the surface, he seemed calm, almost to the point of being self-effacing; yet, Luisa and I had seen Joel's hidden anger flare up.

So far, I had managed to avoid considering Reyna's feelings and her children's predicament. What would happen to them? Would she be able to support the family? What if we were wrong and Joel had nothing to do with this mess? Then I had nothing to worry about but political embarrassment, a somewhat comforting thought, considering the other possibilities.

As I walked closer to the front door of the warehouse, the smell of excrement became more pungent. Now I was sure it was coming from an organic source nearby, not from my memory. I followed my nose to a place outside, just a few feet to the right of the door, where streaks of feces were still attracting an occasional fly.

Quite subconsciously, I called on my newly-discovered powers to get more details about the killer, but I couldn't see anything this time. More disappointed by the lack of results than angry at having tried, I turned around and began to walk towards the car. Kenyon had already called for a forensics team to gather evidence, so I told him about the excrement I'd found.

"We have to postpone your visit to the Galeanos' house for a couple of hours. It's important that the forensics team go over everything before you pay a visit to Galeano. Ideally, we would want him to feel that he has to come back here, to the scene of his crime. He might betray something."

"If he does that," I said. "He might come back here out of curiosity. After all, he is a reporter." I saw Kenyon shaking his head, so I added, "You're very sure he killed Mando?"

"As sure as the sun is shining right now." His upper lip stiffened slightly more than usual.

"What makes you so sure? A hunch?" Hearing the challenge in my voice, I shook my head. As difficult as this change in my personality was for me to accept, I had to admit I was becoming a walking contradiction. My emotional reaction to Kenyon's comment and my calling on psychic powers to aid me in identifying the killer attested to my present state of confusion.

"You make it sound as if it were a dirty word." He chuckled.

"I thought detecting was accomplished through the analysis of evidence and lots of legwork. *Ze littel grray cells, mon ami.* Doesn't a detective have to be a combination of Hercule Poirot and Phillip Marlowe?" I tapped at my temple with my index finger. Laid up with a broken foot during my first summer in high school, I had read most of Agatha Christie's and Raymond Chandler's detective novels. But Matthew Kenyon was far from resembling in attitude or appearance either of the two fictional detectives. "Do you really believe in hunches?"

"Don't you?" He peered into my eyes, making me feel uncomfortable. *So, Gloria, you're still afraid of your powers*, his eyes seemed to be saying. A ridiculous assumption, since he had no way of knowing about my flying experience.

"I hate it when people answer a question with a question," I responded without waiting for his reaction. Turning, I headed back to the warehouse.

"Don't touch anything," he warned. "And come back out when you're ready. We have to talk about your visit to the Galeanos' house."

I changed my mind and walked back towards him.

"I just finished talking to my partner," he began telling me. "Money has been exchanged. The Galeanos gave a $25,000 down-payment for the house they live in now."

"When did they do that?"

"About a month ago. The house was registered in the name of Sylvia Castañeda, Galeano's mother-in-law." Kenyon began to perspire. He took a couple of pills out of the vial and popped them into his mouth. This time he didn't try to hide his action from me. He swallowed the pills, then continued, "And we've only started to dig. I'll bet his bank account reveals a great deal of activity in the past few weeks." He wiped the sweat from his forehead with his handkerchief. "Galeano only does free lancing for newspapers. He couldn't possibly put together that much money within a short time. Since he doesn't have a regular job, a bank would look at his savings accounts, credit history and other property to guarantee the mortgage. Maybe that's why he decided to have Sylvia Castañeda apply for the loan. But I think we can safely assume that there was a lot more money involved.

"Then, as I told you, last night, a few minutes after I signaled my partner with the flashlight, he spotted a man who looked like Galeano getting into a car near Saint Augustine's. We're almost sure he didn't know that you and Luisa were there. I think that he had seen Mando going into the yard next to the school playground. Then, when Mando left again, Galeano went after him. McGuire had no idea how important his seeing Galeano at the school area was until this morning, after you, Luisa and I talked about the person who might have killed Mando.

"Remember, if you can't tape your conversation with him, you're not to worry about it. Even if he admitted to the murder or to complicity, we couldn't use that as evidence in court anyway. I'm only hoping that he says something we can use to catch the master mind behind all this. You are not to put yourself at risk needlessly. You're smart, but you're not used to double-dealers like this one. And for God's sake, don't get overconfident!"

He paused. His face was quite devoid of color, the skin around his nose and lips was sallow, and fat drops of sweat had collected around his eyes. He had to be in terrible pain, but he was determined not to let others know about his illness.

"Are you seeing a doctor for your ... condition?" I tried to smile, but I was sure it was only a grimace. I didn't feel very cheery.

He also managed a smile, but I could tell it was costing him dearly. "You make it sound as if I were pregnant."

"Is there anything I can get for you?" I wasn't smiling any more and he stopped pretending about his pain.

"Yes. Get me the killer—the killers." He sighed, and a light wave of color lapped over his cheekbones. The bout was over. "Just tell Galeano that we're going to be combing this area next, gathering hard evidence. That we already suspect someone, but you don't know who it is. Say that I mentioned a greenhouse and old man Preston. Say that you didn't understand half of what I said. Let him pump you for information, but be very careful. You tend to say what's on your mind much too often.

Just let him know what I'm telling you now, and we'll do the rest."

I agreed. Knowing deep inside that Matthew Kenyon was right, I wanted to say a prayer for Joel, but perhaps it was too late and all the prayers in the world couldn't save Mando's killer from himself.

I watched our wavering, foreshortened shadows on the ground—souls caught in a mirage of hell. It was nearly high noon.

ELEVEN

In the Eye of Eyes

Kenyon and I came up La Verne, the street that ended at the Silver Dollar Cafe.

"That's the cafe where Rubén Salazar was killed," I said, pointing at the small one-story building on Whittier Boulevard. Earlier that morning, the Coroner's Office had issued a preliminary report about the death of Rubén Salazar, stating he had died of a wound inflicted by a 9-1/2-inch, rocket-shaped, exploding teargas canister. An inquest would take place in a few days.

"That's where it happened, all right."

"In cases like Rubén Salazar's, does the L.A.P.D. conduct its own investigation?" I asked Kenyon.

"Yes, it usually does. Especially in this case, they'll go to great pains to prove it was a freak accident."

"Is that what you believe?"

"No comment." Kenyon looked at me and smiled. "I'm not interested in either the department's findings or their investigation."

"You talk about the department as if you were not part of it. Don't you like what you do?"

"Yes, but I don't have to like everything about the institution where I do what I like." He looked straight ahead and I took his gesture as my cue to drop the subject.

Kenyon turned right on Whittier Boulevard and we rode in silence until we went past the Galeanos' house. The curtains were drawn in the living room, and there weren't any toys on the porch. Although Joel's car was in the driveway and laundry was drying on the clothesline, there was no sign of activity inside the house.

Kenyon stopped the car a couple of blocks ahead. "Be very careful," he cautioned as I got out and headed for the house. He went to park around the corner.

Those two blocks seemed the longest I'd ever walked. Panting and sweating, I went up the few steps to the front door and rang the bell. No response. I tried the knob. It turned and I pushed the door open.

A sudden gust of warm wind greeted me. Right across from the front door and through a short hall was the back door. It was open. A pungent smell, which became stronger as I approached the fireplace, hung in the air, but I didn't look for its source right then. A loud "hello" didn't afford me a response. No one was in the yard either.

Something unusual was definitely going on. At first, I wasn't sure what it was I was sensing, until I noticed that some objects in particular were missing. Reyna's miniature carvings, which she had shown to me and talked about in detail, were gone from the mantlepiece. The children's toys, Mario's favorite toy train engine and Vida's doll, were not in plain view as they had been the previous times I'd been there.

The fireplace felt unusually warm, and a sharp odor seemed to be coming from it. A closer look at the ashes on the grill told me they were the burnt remnants of photographs and negatives. Whoever had set them on fire hadn't realized the danger of burning so much photo paper in an open fireplace and inside a closed house. Being a photographer, Joel would definitely know about this danger. He had probably opened the back door to air the place. But where was he now?

Not all of the photographs had been reduced to ashes, I noticed, as I removed a few of the pieces. In my eagerness to take them out quickly, I hit my head on the firescreen, knocking my upper and lower teeth against each other. Pain zigzagged up my cheeks; its sharpness brought tears to my eyes. Before I turned to the photo fragments again, I rubbed my forehead and wiped my eyes with my fingers.

Brick steps leading up to a southern style house were pictured in one of the photos; other fragments showed the feet or heads of men in combat uniforms or fatigues. A much younger Joel appeared in one of them. Then my heart jumped when I saw the legs of a child with only a sock and shoe partly visible. It was definitely little Michael's leg. Someone was carrying him. It was impossible to tell much except that the person holding him was wearing black pants. A kind of embroidered insignia, or perhaps a brand label, was barely distinguishable on the back pocket.

The Galeanos kept an assortment of supplies in the breakfast nook, and I looked inside for a magnifying glass to examine the emblem on the pants, but couldn't find one. Since Joel developed his own photographs, he would probably keep a magnifying glass where he processed the films, I figured, so I began to look for his darkroom.

I moved around the house fast and quietly. After a brief, unsuccessful search, I went out the back door. Outside, I found the entrance to the basement. My hand was already on the doorknob when I heard the front door slam. I quickly put the scraps of the photos into a pocket on my vest, pushed the record button on the cassette recorder, and double-checked the right pocket on my jeans to make sure I still had the transmitter. My hand was shaking visibly, so I kept it in the pocket of my jeans. The feel of the transmitter renewed my confidence, and I headed to the house and paused at the back door.

Joel was standing in the middle of the kitchen, his back to me. My knocking on the door startled him and he turned around quickly. I gasped. A large piece of gauze was secured with adhesive tape on the left side of his jaw, and a few scratches on his cheek showed up above the bandage.

"My God, what happened to you?" I said.

"Gloria! What are you doing here?" His voice betrayed more surprise than concern.

"I knocked, but there was no answer. The front door was unlocked and the back door was open." I stayed where I was beside the door. "Were you in an accident?"

He sat down and broke into tears. The whole scene was entirely different from the one I'd imagined when Kenyon and I were riding down the boulevard. My first impulse was to go to him and console him, but I held back. After a few minutes, he quieted down, got up, reached for a tissue from the box on the counter and blew his nose.

"I'm sorry," said Joel. "It's been a terrible day."

"Insufferable three days if you ask me," I said. It seemed so easy to be there, talking to this man, as if we were old friends. He seemed so vulnerable, and all I was able to feel for him was pity. The mire was quickly becoming a swamp, a voice inside me warned.

"I know. Rubén's death. The riot. Now this." He touched the bandage over his jaw lightly.

"What happened?"

If any of this had to do with little Michael's death, I knew he wouldn't break down and tell me about it. Regret but no fear appeared in his eyes; mostly pain circled in his gaze.

"Reyna's left me. She took the kids this morning and left. *Esa cabrona.*" He hit the kitchen table with his fist, making my heart jump as high as the sugar bowl. "She also cleaned out our bank accounts."

Joel reached for the scissors. I wanted to scream or press the transmitter's red button, but I controlled myself. "She took these," he said, holding the scissors as if they were a knife and cutting the air with them.

"And she slashed my face with them."

This visit was beginning to be more than I'd bargained for. I had to steer the conversation away from our present subject.

Joel sat down and put the scissors on the table.

"What a terrible thing to happen," I said. "First the death of your friend, and now this thing with Reyna." Regaining control of myself and the situation, and not wanting to give him time to react to my comments, I added, "I was with Matthew Kenyon earlier this morning. He told me there's going to be an inquiry into Rubén Salazar's death soon."

Joel looked up but he seemed to be having a hard time focusing. I went to the stove, picked up the teapot, filled it with water and put it on one of the front burners. "I'll make you some coffee," I said. "Or do you prefer tea?" My hand was a lot steadier. "How sad, this thing with Reyna." I said hoping to gain time.

"It's so ironic. She's been upset because I don't have a steady job. 'The kids want this. My mother needs that.' Always nagging me. Hey, I don't wanna go work in a photo lab. I wanna write for a newspaper, make a living as a photographer. *Pero esa* wouldn't hear of it. '*Dame, dame!* Gimme, gimme!' That's all she knows. *Por fin* I give her, *y bastante.*" He got up and leaned on the counter. "But it wasn't enough."

"It seems to me you provide well for her and the kids. I mean, you live comfortably and she doesn't have to work, does she?"

"She didn't have to worry about anything anymore." He became agitated and began to shift his eyes around. I didn't say anything. "She slashed my face and took off in her car." He paused. "She's not at her mother's. I went to her friend Becky's house, a few blocks away on Atlantic Avenue, but she hadn't seen my wife or my kids." He touched the bandage. "I've done all this shit for her and the kids, and now ... "

"What shit?" I wanted to ask, but I refrained. Since the coffee was ready, I poured a cup for him and one for myself. Then, we sat down at the table.

"It seems that everything happens at once," I began, "Matthew Kenyon told me Mando was killed last night." I waited for Joel's reaction, but he kept stirring his coffee, apparently engrossed by the rivulets that formed when he moved the spoon in the opposite direction. I took a sip, then continued, "He thinks that Mando was murdered because he could identify little Michael's killer." If Kenyon was on the right track, Joel would know the murderer's reasons for wanting Mando dead as well. I expected him to confirm this, but he gave no sign of even hearing me.

I had the feeling that the tables had turned. But I couldn't stop at that point without arousing suspicion. "Anyway, Kenyon thinks there are two killers. He gave me all sorts of theories, but I'm not sure I understand everything he said." Praying all the time that my hand wouldn't shake so much that I'd spill the coffee, I drank the rest of it in three long gulps, then got up and put the cup in the sink. Out of habit, I took my keys out and turned to leave.

"I'm sorry, Gloria," Joel said. "You were telling me something. Who got killed?"

More terrifying than having watched him thrust the scissors in the air was the sound of his voice now, composed and unfeeling. It was no longer the painful voice of a man lamenting the loss of his family. I imagined his eyes looking coldly at my back, his mind ready for the next question, planning the next move. I was glad I wasn't facing him, or he would have been able to notice the fear and confusion in my eyes. I put the keys in my vest pocket and turned around. His eyes drifted over my face as if he were looking at me for the first time. Then he fixed his gaze on mine. The game had begun and it was going to be a difficult one.

"I was telling you that Mando was killed last night."

"How?" He took his time asking the second question. "Where was he killed?"

How and where, but not who? An interesting omission and the one to be pursued. So I said, "Kenyon seems to think that the man who killed Mando is not the same one who killed the little boy."

A touch of apprehension moved swiftly across his eyes as Joel asked, "What makes Kenyon think there are two killers?"

"The very different ways in which Mando and Michael were killed. The Modus Operandi. Is that the way it's said?" Distract and survive, I thought. "Luisa's all excited. She thinks it's a conspiracy."

Joel hadn't insisted on knowing just how Mando had been killed, which meant that perhaps he was measuring my strength before proceeding. Then he asked, "What do *you* think?"

I held his gaze, then sighed and looked away. My stomach began to feel empty. "I don't know what to think, to tell you the truth. I don't understand half the things that are happening. But I guess Matthew Kenyon does."

"What did he tell you?" His voice remained unchanged. He served himself some more coffee.

"Well, basically that's it. That little Michael Cisneros and Mando were killed by two different people."

He sat at the table again. "Does he have any clue as to who killed them or why they were killed?"

Gambit. Black queen stands alone. The white pawn savors victory.

The words bounced in my mind. "He didn't tell me," I answered, "but he did tell me that he'll probably have Mando's killer in custody by this evening at the latest."

Giving Joel the information he needed afforded me a certain degree of control over him. But the real power resided in my letting him think he had control over me. Otherwise, the gambit was not possible.

"Oh? So Kenyon knows who this murderer is?" He casually drank from his cup, but he didn't take his eyes off me.

"As I said, he didn't tell me whom he suspects, but I think he's closing in on someone. He was waiting for a warrant so he could check out some sort of ... greenhouse ... near here, I think. But he may not get the warrant until late this afternoon." Most likely from suppressing my fear for so long, I was beginning to feel lightheaded. I also felt utterly alone.

"So there's no connection between the two killings after all?"

By looking at Joel I had difficulty telling whether or not he was apprehensive. Leaning back, he rocked lightly in his chair.

"I'm not sure, but I believe Kenyon thinks there *is* a connection," I said. "How did he put it? Yes. He said that little Michael's killer is the mastermind."

A sardonic smile crossed Joel's face, but he didn't say anything. He was calm, too calm. This was perhaps the time to leave. I looked at the clock; it had been forty minutes since I'd first set foot in that house.

"She burned all the photographs and the negatives, too. *La cabrona.* You saw them, there, in the fireplace. That was our insurance. Even though he promised we'd be set for life, I didn't believe him. It's always better to have some sort of insurance." Joel's face was flushed.

"He?"

Immediately, I regretted my question, but it was too late. I wanted to run out of there, but walked away instead, as calmly as possible. The chair where he'd been sitting crashed to the floor. In two strides he was behind me. My arms and legs tingled as blood rushed through them, but my mind was fixed on one thing only, getting out of there. I kept on walking.

Joel opened a cupboard while I rushed through the door and into the hall that led to the living room. I heard the click as he released the safety of the gun. A .38 revolver, Kenyon would later tell me.

I reached for the transmitter, but my jeans were tight and I had to use both my hands to pull it out. I felt I didn't have a grip on it.

A clicking noise told me Joel had snapped on the safety again. "Thank you" almost escaped from me.

"They took me to Rio, first class all the way," Joel was saying. "I felt we were all brothers. They wanted a better world for our kids. I wanted that, too. The gangs—they take kids and turn them into *chucos, tecatos,* thieves."

I couldn't make much sense of what he was saying.

"Who ... ?" I asked him, hoping to find out who had sought his assistance. I felt the muzzle of the gun sliding down my left side. Joel grabbed me by the hair. He rapped on the tape recorder with the barrel of the gun. "Just like Reyna. You, too, Gloria. *Traidoras. Todas.* You women are all traitors. I killed one of the Santos for her. That's how much I loved her and ... she said she wanted to throw up when she saw the photos, that she hated me," he whimpered. "She's to blame for everything. You and I are going to die and she's the one to blame ... she's the guilty one."

"You and I are going to die." Was that what he had said?

Joel let go of me just long enough for me to get to the tape recorder. He was holding me by the hair but my hands were free. I managed to yank the transmitter out and quickly pressed the red button. He didn't notice it and let go of my hair. With one hand he was holding the gun, and with the other he was jerking at the recorder, pulling it from under my blouse. Then he smashed it against the wall as he grabbed my arm and turned me around to face him. For the first time, I saw the gun pointed at my heart.

I wanted to plead with Joel to turn himself in, to tell Kenyon who the other killer was. But I could only manage a hoarse, unintelligible groan. I felt the muzzle of the gun pressing against my breast. Not wanting Joel's distorted face to be the last memory I'd take with me, I closed my eyes, waiting for the safety to click off. With the eye of eyes, I focused on the images of my mother and father, my husband and daughter, and my friend Luisa. This was the only way I could avoid dying in anguish, alone, far from those I loved.

Suddenly, I heard the front door crash open. I opened my eyes to see Joel taking aim as he pushed me back. Then he changed his mind and began to run for the back door. I fell on my knees, attempting to regain my balance. Kenyon, followed by McGuire, jumped over me in pursuit of Joel. My whole body felt like a sack full of rocks. I struggled for a while before I could stand up and take a few shaky steps. Only a couple of feet from the door to the basement, I heard Kenyon pleading with Joel to give himself up. A few seconds later, I heard a shot.

"Kenyon? Are you all right?" I yelled, half tumbling down the basement steps.

"I'm okay, Gloria. Don't come downstairs. He shot himself." The smell of blood suddenly filled the air. I stopped outside the doorway to the darkroom. Even so, I glimpsed part of Joel's bloody head. As fast as I could, I staggered on, back to the house. Relief, sadness and anger tangled around my heart, as I realized that now we might never really know who killed little Michael. From out in the yard, I heard the loud cry of a cat, the only mourner Joel Galeano deserved.

TWELVE

Bees and Burials

When emotions threaten to overload the nervous system, some people have nosebleeds. Others have spells of melancholy or they stammer. Overloading for me meant an attack of hiccups. In a way, they were a positive release of tension, for they were neither painful nor dangerous. None of the usual remedies worked for me. My attacks lasted about fifteen minutes, the time it took for all the pent-up energy to be freed. But for Luisa, as for other people around me, my hiccups were a matter of concern.

When Luisa found out about my encounter with Joel, she asked for the afternoon off and walked over to the Galeanos' house just as I was experiencing the hiccups attack. She was hardly through the door when she was already running to the kitchen to get me a glass of water. I dutifully sipped it to please her. She then dipped a tissue in the leftover water and wiped my forehead and right cheek with it. When I looked at the splotches of wet ash on the towel, I felt truly stupid. Joel had known all along I'd been sticking my nose into the fireplace.

"He could have killed me, but he didn't," I said to Luisa after I recounted the events leading up to my confrontation with Joel.

"Perhaps he was temporarily insane," Luisa offered. "And that prevented him from killing you."

At first, her explanation seemed irrational, but, on second thought, I realized she might be right. For Joel, in an odd way, killing Mando had been a business affair, a logical and rational act. He had wanted to eradicate gangs. By a twist of logic, little Michael's cunning murderer had given Joel the opportunity to do so, even rewarding him generously for his action, thus closing the circle around him. Joel had thought that this reward would in turn earn him the respect and undying gratitude of his wife and children. But it hadn't worked out that way, and nothing had made any sense to him after Reyna's violent disapproval.

87

Perhaps Luisa was right; yet, I wanted to believe that Joel had spared my life as a last effort to regain self-respect.

Except for some bruises on my back and a slightly tattered soul, I felt grateful to walk out of the Galeanos' house in one piece. But I was angry at Joel for having killed himself, thus taking the identity of little Michael's killer with him. I was equally upset at myself for not probing, for conforming instead to the rules Kenyon had set for me. On the other hand, it was now evident that I hadn't been a match for Joel. Could I possibly imagine that I could ever outwit the other killer—the mastermind—who left nothing to chance?

Perhaps Kenyon had been right all along, and I should just go back to Oakland, leaving these matters of detection to him. But he himself had gathered so little evidence that it would take a long time, if not a miracle, to solve little Michael's murder.

Time was what Kenyon no longer had, I thought, watching him during the Mass which commemorated little Michael's short life. After the events at the Galeanos' house, I had taken a tranquilizer, and my recollections of what happened at the church were a bit fuzzy; nonetheless, I had been aware that pain had been Kenyon's constant companion throughout the service.

At the church, during his moments of relief, Kenyon had observed Lillian Cisneros attentively. What was so interesting about her? I wondered. True, she was beautiful. Dark and round, but not fat. She was a couple of inches taller and perhaps even a few years older than Luisa and me. Her long hair was pulled back in a single tight braid. Under the short black veil, her oval face showed a complexion unblemished, except by the reddish marks grief had temporarily left around her eyes and on the tip of her nose. There wasn't any particularly attractive feature about her if one observed each part individually. But viewed in her entirety, she was pleasing to look at. She had what my grandmother used to refer to as a classical look. Women like Lillian Juárez Cisneros were groomed usually to be the wives of rich and powerful men. Was this the woman Kenyon was observing so assiduously? Or was it the vulnerable young woman who had been found lying next to the *Pietà* fountain blaming herself for her son's death?

My thoughts shifted to Michael Cisneros, to the way he'd looked, standing beside his wife. The impression I'd gotten when I first shook his hand was that of a very old soul in a body no older than thirty-three—the same age as Darío. Perhaps I had this impression because of his quiet voice and gentle manner. Perhaps because of the soft look of his honey-colored eyes under long, straight lashes and well-shaped eyebrows. Michael Cisneros wasn't meek-looking by any means, but his unobtrusive demeanor was hardly what anyone would expect from the president of a company that had considerably widened its scope, quadrupling its profit in the two years under his direction. To what extent had he been the *real* target for little Michael's murderer, I wondered. Or to what extent had the target been Paul, Michael's brother?

Paul had also had something to do with this unusual growth in the company, I figured. He was definitely his brother's right hand and his most trusted partner, but his power was limited by the fact that he owned only thirty percent of Black Swan Enterprises. Paul was charming, outgoing and quite a public relations man, Otilia had told me. He seemed to be just the right person to head the company's expansion program under his brother's leadership.

It was difficult to tell whether it'd been Lillian, Michael or Paul Cisneros who had attracted the envy or the contempt of little Michael's killer. All three seemed so poised and successful. Yet, any one of them inadvertently could have done something to someone, which then assumed great importance to the injured party. Had this person nurtured such strong negative feelings for so long that they had turned into a searing hatred, into the kind of energy it takes to want to kill a four-year-old child?

Later, as I slipped into a warm tub at Luisa's apartment, I considered the chances for the murderer to ever be apprehended. Clues as to the killer's identity had obviously been burned by Reyna. The rest had died with Joel Galeano. As hard as it was to accept, I would perhaps have to learn to live with the idea that the murder would never be solved. What would I do then with my visions, with the pieces of photos I had in my vest pocket, and other odds and ends of information I held in my brain? Three people were dead, and I had personally met two of them if only for a brief time.

The warm bubble bath followed by a short nap had finally helped me regain some of my physical and mental strength. This Monday, August 31, was moving closer to its appointed end, as inexorably as the lives of Michael David Cisneros, Mando and Joel Galeano had taken their appointed routes.

I opened my eyes to see Luisa sitting at her desk, her chin resting on her open palm. She was so still that for a moment I thought she had fallen asleep. But then her left hand moved rhythmically across a sheet of paper. She was writing a poem, I knew.

Piel canela y ojos de gato—Cinnamon skin and cat's eyes. That's how Mami Julia used to describe Luisa. Her mother's family was from somewhere in the state of Jalisco, Mexico, where, Mrs. Cortez had told me, many people have Danish and Mexican ancestry. This might be why many of the natives of that area have green or blue eyes. Luisa's eyes were round and green. Back in elementary school, I used to describe the color of her eyes as yellow, and corrected everyone who said otherwise.

After fourth grade, Luisa and I had spent a whole summer comparing notes on the color of things around us and getting into arguments about what we had seen. We could never settle our differences since I couldn't see through her eyes nor she through mine. When she recalled people and things, her descriptions were always vivid and full of details. "Because of your yellow eyes," I'd tell her. Mine were dark brown, and for years, I was also convinced that the color of my eyes had a lot to do with my having an "impressionable mind," a taste for the dark.

The first time Luisa let me read her poetry we were seventeen and about to finish high school. She laughed when I told her she was a poet because her eyes were yellow. I felt that two contrastive personas clearly existed in Luisa, for I had never known anyone who found so much humor in everything she experienced; yet, she could turn around and write incredibly melancholic poems. Poetry was the element that brought harmony into her life, that made everything endurable, she once told me.

I was beginning to see some similarities between Luisa and me, but they in no way related to poetry. Rather, I seemed to have developed two incongruous sides to my personality, each constantly confronting the other now. Unlike Luisa, I hadn't yet discovered how to make both aspects of myself work in harmony. When things quieted down, I would have to work at this, I thought, as I closed my eyes and my mind began to drift.

First there was silence, interrupted by flashes of color. Then a melody began taking form. A soprano voice began to sing a haunting, doleful song, the words coming out of my memory like bees made of light flying towards their honeycomb. It was a song from an opera, I was sure, but I couldn't place it. It made me think of the butterfly I had looked at early that morning, of Lillian and Luisa's poems, of honey and lemon, and of that cemetery at the foot of the misty hills of Oakland where little Michael David would rest for all eternity. Perhaps it was time to go home, to bury the knowledge of death with the corpses, and go on with the business of living as best I could.

THIRTEEN

Familia de Santos/Family of Woman

It was early evening on Tuesday, September 1, 1970, when Luisa and I got to Mando's house on Rosa Street. In this part of East Los Angeles, without the preamble of chain-link fences or front lawns, the street intruded with all its noise and violence directly into people's living rooms. The only greenery was the jagged anise plants that sprung stubbornly from the cracks in the sidewalk.

"I'm Gloria Damasco," I said to the woman who answered the door. She was about my age, hence I assumed she was Mando's sister. The six-month-old girl sitting astride her hip threw her arms up and greeted us with a wet, dimply smile, while the young woman looked us over. "This is my friend Luisa Cortez," I added. "We knew Mando."

"*Sí*, Gloria. *Claro*. Come in. I'm Cecilia Cadena," she said while she walked to the playpen and got the baby settled in it. "Okay, Little Sister, don't fuss. No. Stay there."

Luisa and I looked at each other. We had assumed the two were mother and daughter.

"What's your daughter's name?" Luisa asked, still wanting to clarify their relationship.

"She's my sister. Beni. Benita." Cecilia gave the child a pacifier, even though she was quite placidly sucking on her own hand. "Mando talked to me about you. You were the ones who found the dead boy, *no*?" She gulped in some air, which an instant later came out in broken sighs. "I'm so glad that son of a bitch is dead—that man, what's his name?"

"Joel Galeano," Luisa offered.

"I'm glad he killed himself. And that he died like a street dog, all alone. But I know that won't bring Mando back. Nothing will." She held the tip of her nose between index and thumb while inhaling through it.

I felt a kinship with Cecilia immediately, perhaps because, as had

91

been my experience, she was expected to look after the younger children in the family. As Luisa pointed out later, we were about the same age and, although we really didn't resemble each other, we could have passed for sisters. Undoubtedly, she had been the member of the family closest to Mando and that was why he had trusted me.

The parched skin on her eyelids and the feverish brilliance of her eyes attested to her long hours of crying, but she was now past the point of tears. For all practical purposes, we soon found out, Cecilia was in charge of the household, since her mother was the sole wage-earner. Cecilia also was responsible for solving any problems that might arise concerning her brother and her baby sister.

I looked around the small living room and at the photographs of the family on the TV console: the usual family assemblage—black-and-whites of Mando and Cecilia as babies, pictures of their mother; color prints of Cecilia's *Quinceañera*, of Mando at six and at fifteen, and of baby Benita. No wedding pictures, though, not even a snapshot of a man.

Luisa played with Beni for awhile, then she joined us. "She's a happy, good-natured baby," she told Cecilia. "You take good care of her."

"Thanks. My mom works six days a week. She's the cashier at the Jardines de Villa Restaurant on Sunset. They let her take the day off yesterday, but today she had to go to work. Right now I only have a part-time job in the morning right here in East Los, so I can help with Beni." Cecilia looked at the photographs on the console. "Mando was so good with her. He used to take care of her while I was at work."

"I didn't know your brother well, but I could tell he was a good person—a decent young man," I said.

"Yeah, he was." Cecilia smiled. She had a beautiful smile.

Luisa then asked Cecilia the question I too wondered about: "Was Mando a member of the Santos for a long time?"

"He was. Lately, he'd been thinking about dropping out." Beni was beginning to whimper. Cecilia looked at her watch. "C'mon into the kitchen. Gotta get her food ready."

Luisa took up the task of pursuing the subject of the Santos and Mando's membership in the gang. From past experiences, I suspected she had a notion she wanted to prove or disprove. "How come Mando wanted to drop out of the gang?"

Cecilia looked at Luisa, then at me. She had a knowing smile. "You probably think that gangs are all *malos, no*? Not so. At least *los Santos* weren't that bad. Not till a few months ago, anyway." She filled a pan with water and, putting Benita's bottle in it, set it on the burner to warm up the formula. "Some gangs, like the Santos, are like a *familia*. Real close-knit. *Muy unidos.* They protect and support each other. The Santos were good for Mando. You see, my father left us when Mando was born. But, at a certain age, Mando needed to be around a man so he could learn how to be a man. Some of the older Santos were like a father to him, always there for him. They're changing now, though. That's what Mando had been telling me lately. I'm not sure he knew why." Cecilia went into the living room to pick up Benita.

"Maybe it's true that most gangs will eventually become violent . . . maybe that's what's happening to the Santos," I suggested.

"Yeah." Cecilia responded, as he walked back into the kitchen. "I don't exactly know why. Maybe they're afraid of other gangs. Before, no one would dare come into the neighborhood. In a way, the Santos protected us. But now . . . "

"Maybe the cops are after them now," Luisa offered.

"No," she said, shrugging her shoulders. "The cops have always been after them. Something else is going on. *Andan un poco locos.* Real crazy."

"Drugs?" I suggested.

Cecilia shook her head. "They've always done some grass, but nothing else. The Santos are not real *vatos locos.* The *vatos locos* are the dudes who'll try anything they can get their hands on. They'll shoot up, smoke, drink or snort—everything and anything. But *los Santos*? Nah."

"Let me feed her," Luisa said when the baby's bottle was ready. Cecilia checked Luisa out for a moment. Then, she handed Luisa both the baby and the bottle.

"To tell you the truth," I said after a while, "I've heard a lot about what goes on in gangs and the Santos just sound too good to be true."

Cecilia stared at me, then I suppose she decided it was all right for me to talk that way. "I'm not defending them just because. The Santos have done a lot of good, like for the older people. I mean, *los viejitos* never feared walking out on the street alone when the Santos were around." She grabbed the kitchen towel and wiped the sweat from Benita's forehead and neck. "I know they may do *Dios sabe cuánto más.* But no. They aren't dealing drugs. They're becoming like a real army, with heavy guns, like those used in war. I don't know anything about guns—never even seen one—but that's what Mando told me."

"In some way they function like an army, don't they? I mean, the way they guard their territory," Luisa commented, then added, "Members of the same gang wear the same uniform, right?"

"If I remember correctly," I stated, "the Santos' uniform is a black leather vest with a skull and halo painted on the back, and black pants.

Mando wasn't wearing a shirt, so I'm assuming that in the summer the Santos don't wear shirts, right?"

"Yeah," Cecilia answered. "Wearing their uniform helps the members recognize each other right away, anywhere."

"Would anyone who's not a gang member be allowed to wear that gang's uniform?" I asked. When Cecilia shook her head, I continued, "Did Mando ever tell you about anyone who was going around dressed like the Santos? I mean someone who was *not* a member of the group?"

"Yeah," Cecilia answered without hesitating, "but Mando himself saw only one such character. That tall dude who was carrying the little boy. Mando mentioned it to El Lucio. He's Mando's padrino and an important member of the Santos," she explained. "He's a nice man, with all kinds of *conexiones en el barrio* and beyond. But not even El Lucio could find out who this tall dude was. The Santos will nab him if they ever see him again. But it's like he was here, then he was gone, *como de rayo.* Just like that." She snapped her fingers and Benita let go of the nipple and giggled.

"Why didn't the Santos protect Mando?" I knew there was anger in my voice but I didn't try to hide it.

"I've asked myself that question also," Cecilia said as she nodded. "But don't go blaming them. I mean ... Mando didn't tell them all he knew. Even El Lucio wasn't aware of all that Mando had seen. My brother didn't want to get the other Santos involved." She swallowed a couple of times, then added, "And I *really* didn't think he was in danger."

"Don't go blaming yourself. You've done more than anyone could expect," Luisa said with such fervor that Cecilia blushed.

"Did Mando tell you what that man, the one who was carrying little Michael, looked like? Did he describe him to you?" My heart was beating fast.

"Mando said that dude was about a head taller than him, and Mando was five feet six. So like the dude's about six-feet tall, on the slim side, Mando said, and he was wearing a wig, and a fake moustache." She looked at the baby, who had finished her bottle and was dozing off in Luisa's arms. Picking Benita up, Cecilia went to lay her down in her crib.

Luisa and I waited for her in silence, almost as if we both felt that if we talked, we would break her train of thought.

"Mando followed him," Cecilia said as she walked back into the kitchen. "He had been watching the riot from a liquor store across from the Silver Dollar Cafe. You know that cafe? Where that cop killed Rubén Salazar?"

I indicated we knew where the cafe was. Then, Luisa asked, "Was Mando there before or at the time Rubén Salazar was killed?"

"Some time before," Cecilia said, and after a brief moment, she continued, "Well, he saw this stranger dressed like the Santos with a child in his arms, and he began to follow him. That Joel Galeano—he came out of the cafe a couple of seconds after the tall dude went by. Mando said he noticed Galeano because he was taking photos. But he didn't know exactly because the camera was covering his face most of the time. My brother told me that's why he didn't recognize Galeano right away when he saw him with you, after you found the little boy."

"Michael David Cisneros was the boy's name," Luisa whispered.

"Michael David," Cecilia said the name in a soft voice. After a moment she continued: "The crowd was pushing back when those pigs started shooting gas. Mando told me that he had also heard a gunshot. But our neighbor Tobias was there too, across the street from the cafe and he says no gun shots were fired into the cafe where Rubén Salazar was. Anyway, Mando kept following the tall dude. He noticed that the little boy wasn't moving, that he was limp. Lots of people were running from the police and the gas. Someone pushed Mando. Suddenly, he and the tall dude were that close." Cecilia indicated the length of an inch between her index and thumb. "The stranger looked straight at Mando, and Mando was close enough to see a scar on the stranger's arm. But Mando said the scar looked fake, too."

"Do you know of anyone else who saw this man?" I asked on the off chance someone else had reported seeing him.

"Our neighbor Tobias mentioned he'd seen Mando with another member of the Santos, but he really didn't pay much attention." Cecilia shrugged her shoulders. "Who has time to look around when the *pigs* get wild?"

"I know." I shivered at the memory of the shrieking, the smell of blood and the stink of tear gas.

"Did the tall dude notice Mando following him?" Luisa asked, trying to steer the conversation back to the subject at hand.

"Mando didn't think so," Cecilia answered, "but he wasn't sure. The crowd was pushing hard, and he lost the guy. Then, when Mando was crossing Marigold Street, he saw the same boy lying on the sidewalk. He became suspicious about the tall dude but he didn't know what to do. So he waited at the corner. I think he was hoping that the little boy would wake up. Finally, he decided to go up to the boy and shake him."

"Did he tell you he found a newspaper clipping?" I asked.

"Yeah. But it didn't make any sense to him."

"How come he didn't call the police or one of the Santos?"

"Are you kidding? Santos never call the police. Mando would of gotten into trouble if he had. He had to wait until someone discovered the body. He told me he was so relieved when you two came across it. But then you came back with that man, that Galeano."

"Something doesn't make sense here," I said. "When I got to the Galeanos' house, Joel was there. But you say that Mando recognized Joel when he came back with me, as the man with the camera who had taken pictures of the murderer, right?"

"That's what Mando said. He also told me that the guy who turned out to be Galeano disappeared before Mando got to Marigold Street, but he was absolutely sure that this Galeano was aware of what the other dude had done. The Santos knew that Galeano wanted the police to wipe out the gangs, but they didn't consider him *de cuidado*—you know—not real dangerous." She sucked in her breath, then tried to hold back the tears. "Not real dangerous!"

Cecilia had been sitting across from me at the kitchen table and I put my hand on hers. "I'm sorry. I'm really sorry," I said. "In some ways I feel responsible for what happened to Mando."

"Why? Did you know Galeano was going to kill my brother?" Her tone was harsh. Although I was sure she hadn't intended it, her question sounded like a reproach.

"No," I said. "I didn't know Joel was involved in all this. I was supposed to meet Mando at Saint Augustine School. I didn't know Detectives Kenyon and McGuire were following us, so I wasn't able to talk to your brother. You see, Kenyon and I had discussed a better deal for Mando and I was supposed to tell him about it. But because I had been careless in letting the policemen follow us, I never had a chance to talk to Mando about the offer. If we had been able to talk maybe ... "

"I don't think Mando blamed you for that."

"You mean you saw him after our meeting at the school yard?" That possibility was something I hadn't expected. Neither had Luisa, who looked at me with surprise.

"Uh-huh," Cecilia sighed loudly. "He came by to pick up a jacket and a change of clothes. He told me what had happened, but he said he was going to look for you again."

"Where was he going? Did he tell you?"

"No, he didn't say that much. In his own way, he was trying to protect me. But I do know that the Santos have *chantes*, two or three places where they put up the *familia*; but I don't know where they are."

"Who's the *familia*?"

"Any of them. All of them."

I was so tempted to tell Cecilia where one of those places was located, and what had happened to Mando there, that the spasms in my throat quickly became hiccups. Luisa and Cecilia immediately proceeded to put me in the hold-your-breath-and-look-up-while-drinking-water position. I humored them.

"Has Detective Kenyon been by to see you?" Luisa asked Cecilia, giving me a chance to get over the hiccups.

"Oh, yeah. He and another cop have been asking questions all over the neighborhood. First they were after the Santos. But the Santos all know how to keep one step ahead of the cops. Then Kenyon and McGuire came to see me and to ask me about Mando."

"What did you tell them?"

"Nothing. Then this same cop, Kenyon, came over to tell me Mando was dead. I had to identify the body. That other cop, McGuire? He phoned to say that Galeano had killed Mando and then killed himself, too." Cecilia looked down at her hands. "Maybe I should of told these two cops what I knew that first time they came over." She laced her fingers, then put her hands on her chest and shook her head. "How was I to know these two were good cops or, at least, not so bad? You don't know how terrible the cops are around here. I don't know what makes them hate us so much."

Neither Luisa nor I answered. What could we say? I'd taken a calculated risk with Kenyon, on a single occasion. But his good deeds would not erase the bloody footprints left by his fellow cops. That violent Saturday at Laguna Park would stay with all of us forever.

FOURTEEN

The Dreams of the Dead

My father never trusted airplanes. In addition to the prohibitive cost of air travel for a family of five with a single income, the possibility of the plane plunging into a deep blue ocean or a thick green forest terrified him. Since we didn't go any place where he couldn't drive us, I didn't travel by plane until I went back east with Darío to meet his family. For Darío, who came from an upper middle-class Puerto Rican family, air travel was as commonplace as going to the movies. For me, flying would always be a risky affair. And in light of my "flying" experiences lately, I couldn't resist a smile.

Thinking about these things, I walked down the jetway to board the plane back to Oakland. It was Wednesday afternoon, September 2, 1970, and Matthew Kenyon had taken me to the airport. Although I didn't see him when I turned back to say goodbye, I felt his presence still in the waiting area, like the light of a pulsar star in my subconscious.

As had happened with Mando when I saw him on that Sunday night at Saint Augustine's, I knew that Detective Sargeant Matthew Kenyon and I would not meet face to face again.

Earlier in the day, when I went to his office to inform him of my afternoon departure, and to inquire about possible new developments, he had been looking out the window. He glanced at me over his shoulder as he asked me, "Are you doing all right now?" Then he returned to his idle surveillance of the parking lot behind the L.A.P.D.

Kenyon wasn't the kind of man to make small talk. Yet, he was trying very hard to exchange pleasantries with me. It was amusing and sad at the same time, this talk about fog and chilly winds in charming San Francisco, and haze and smog in metropolitan Los Angeles. Weather chit-chat will cover only so much emotional territory, and after a short while, we both stopped talking.

He was the first one to break the silence. "So now you're going back to the Bay Area," he said.

I nodded, sighed and sat down. "I hate to go. So many unanswered questions."

"We're still looking for Reyna Galeano. She's disappeared without a trace, and her mother, Sylvia Castañeda, is not talking." Kenyon turned around and sat on the window sill. "What time are you leaving?"

"Late this afternoon."

"Is Luisa taking you to the airport?" He was fidgety, quite ill-at-ease.

"No. She can't take me," I answered. "She has to work. I'll catch the airport shuttle."

"May I?" He smiled a kind of nervous smile. "Take you?"

"That'd be great. Thanks." His offer made me feel more relaxed.

"I want to ask you something. And I want you to be honest with me." He sat erect on the corner of his desk, his head slightly pushed forward so that he could look at me through his bifocals.

"Ask away," I said to him. "Ask anything you want to know."

"What's your opinion of Lillian Cisneros? I mean—as a woman looking at another woman." He threw a quick glance over my shoulder. I expected to hear someone speak behind me, but no one did.

"She's very refined and very attractive." I was curt. I didn't want to talk about Lillian, not so much out of respect for her personally since I hardly knew her, but because she was little Michael's mother and Otilia's daughter. Kenyon's scrutiny of Lillian at the church and his present inquiry piqued my curiosity. "Do you suspect her or do you want to protect her?" I asked facetiously.

Kenyon shrugged his shoulder, dismissing my comment with his gesture. He turned again to view the parking lot. I felt the pressure of tears around my eyes, like a child whose favorite teacher has scolded her in front of her peers. At the same time, I was angry at myself for letting him, a man *and a cop*, have that kind of authority over me. Why was I allowing him that power?

"She wouldn't kill her own child," I finally said. There was no reaction from him, so I continued: "If she knew who killed him, she would tell you, wouldn't she? As far as I know, she loves her husband ... seems to be a good wife. She probably was a good mother, too. I don't get any bad ... " I hesitated.

Kenyon turned around and smiled at me. "Why don't you say it—*vibes*?"

"I hate fads, linguistic or otherwise." It was good to see him smile, yet I could hardly control my urgency to cry every time I looked at him. Perhaps it was simply my inability to accept that his illness was terminal, but I knew that tightly joined to my denial was a feeling of hopelessness, for this case might never be solved; still, I asked him, "What is it that you suspect about Lillian?"

"I wish I could tell you. The truth is that I don't know. It has to do with what she told her mother. 'What have I done?' That's it. That bothers me." He raised his eyebrows and looked at me as if he expected me to share his suspicion.

It took me a moment to respond—mostly to check myself for any subconscious doubt I might have fostered, but none came to mind. I thought of the butterfly and Lillian's face, and of the song I somehow connected with her. But, how could I tell him about those things? Trying to remain logical and to offer a possible explanation, I said, "She meant that she should have been there with her child instead of at the march."

"That's what I thought when you first told me about it."

"But now you think there's more to it."

"I'm almost sure. It bothers the ... " He shook his head.

"What exactly bothers you?" I heard the door open behind me. I turned around and saw Todd, the cop who had assisted Kenyon and the coroner on Saturday when the police first got involved in little Michael's murder. He was standing at the door, waving a couple of file folders. Kenyon asked him to come in.

"This is all I could find," Todd said. "The Feds mostly have stuff on him, and it's little at that. They have even less on her. McGuire and I have talked to some of their friends and relatives except for Michael Cisneros' brother who's still in Germany. But we haven't picked up much information about the Cisneros. Everything we've got is in there." He handed the file jackets to Kenyon, smiled at me, and left.

I realized I didn't know Todd's last name, so I avoided calling him by name when I said goodbye to him.

Then, I turned my attention to Kenyon again. "You're really seriously concerned about her, aren't you?" The surprise in my voice made Kenyon close the folder and look at me.

"I certainly am. But she's not the only one being investigated." Kenyon was again speaking as if he had nothing to do with this *procedure*. "Let's see what we have about Michael ... " he said as he opened up one of the folders.

"Before you go on ... I still don't understand what makes you suspect Lillian. Why are you having her investigated?"

He sat again on the corner of his desk. "You're a mother. Let me run this by you. You leave your daughter with your mother and you trust your mother implicitly. You leave, certain that your mother will not let anything happen to your child. Something does happen. Why not blame your mother instead of yourself?"

"I see what you mean. But it's not a good argument. We mothers are constantly being told that our place is beside the children, always looking after them. I'm here now and my daughter is in Oakland with my husband. He takes good care of her, I'm sure, but I still feel guilty for not being there with her. Besides, Lillian's been carrying some kind of guilt, it seems, for a long time. In some irrational way she felt responsible for her father's death. Then her son gets killed. I'm no psychiatrist, but I think she feels she's paying for something."

"Maybe so. This is the FBI dossier on Michael Cisneros, Jr. ... "

"So, they do have a dossier on each one of us." A spontaneous comment on my part which he judiciously ignored at first.

"You shouldn't flatter yourselves. J. Edgar Hoover has files even on his mother and himself." Kenyon chuckled as he flipped through the pages of the file. He adjusted his glasses, then said, "Michael Cisneros must have a history of something or other for the Feds to have been concerned with him. What I'm interested in is information about the family and his personal background.

"How do you get all that information about people?"

"All the personal and family data we got from relatives, friends, immediate family, and from Lillian and Michael Cisneros themselves. We also put in a request to the Feds and they sent us what they had."

"So you put together a profile from two files."

He answered with a nod, then silently began to go over the information, reading aloud from the file and editorializing as he went along.

"Born on May 5, 1937, in Mexico City while his parents lived there. He was given the name of Michael Cisneros, Jr. His father, born Miguel Eduardo Cisneros Belho, changed his name to Michael Cisneros after he came to the United States. Cisneros Sr. was from a well-to-do family that fled Mexico during the Mexican Revolution—1921 or thereabouts— went back years later—in the late thirties—as an executive with the Ford Motor Company. He and his wife, Karen Bjorgun-Smith, lived in Puebla and registered Michael Jr. with the American Embassy as an American citizen, on June 10, 1937. A year later, Michael Cisneros Sr.'s father died and left him the family businesses—three hardware stores and two lumber mills in northern California.

"Here's Jr.'s military record. Interesting. He had a 1-A classification when he was a student but no record of his being called to military duty at any time. Hmmmm. Suddenly, a 4-F is granted. No explanation offered, except that an agent ... Peterson, notes some strings might have been pulled by the Bjorgun family, people well-connected socially and politically. Also financially influential."

"When was his classification changed? Was he already married then?" A minute later I answered my own question. "1956–1960? Wasn't that about the time he was in college?" I paused, then concluded, "It's interesting that the FBI investigated the Bjorgun-Cisneros family?"

J. Edgar Hoover, like the Lord, I thought, moved in mysterious ways. But Kenyon had an idea different from mine.

"If they were well-connected politically and were rich, that might have been reason enough for Hoover to check on them. But there's nothing here about that yet."

"What did Michael Jr. do after he graduated?"

"I'm coming to that." Matthew Kenyon continued reading, "Michael Jr. graduated from Harvard in Business Administration, travelled through Europe for awhile, then went to work for his father until ... Ah, here's a possible reason why a file on him was started. He spent about two years in the Peace Corps, first in Colombia, then in Chile. He came back to the U.S. in 1964, to the University of California at Berkeley to get an M.B.A. He became quite active in the Free Speech Movement and other political student activities at Berkeley, another reason why the F.B.I. might have become interested in his activities. Here, let's look at the interviews ... "

Reading quickly through a few more pages, Kenyon found the information he seemed to be looking for. Then he said, "Mother seemed to always come to son Michael's defense, even against her husband's mandates. Even though Michael Jr. did well in school, and had a desire to follow in his father's footsteps, Mr. Cisneros disapproved of his son's involvement in student politics at Berkeley. Father and son quarrelled, but Mr. Cisneros finally forgave his son at his wife's insistance. After his graduation, Michael Jr. went to work for his father. Everything is forgiven and all's well that ends well."

"Not so fast. When did he meet Lillian?

"Let's see ... that probably would be in her file. Yes, here it is. Barbara Nuncio, Lillian Cisneros' friend, says that in 1964, she and Lillian were students at California State College at Long Beach. They attended a state-wide student conference at U.C.L.A., which was also attended by Paul and Michael Cisneros. Michael was not the first of the brothers to meet Lillian. Actually, Paul Cisneros met Lillian first, dated her a couple of times, but 'there was no spark between them' and both lost interest in one another soon after. By the end of the conference, Paul introduced both Lillian and Barbara to Michael, who took to Lillian immediately.

From then on, Michael travelled regularly to L.A. to see Lillian. They announced their engagement in December, 1964, got married in February of 1965. Michael David was born to them on March 15, 1967."

"Three years later his son's murdered—not so happy an ending after all, is it?" Although Kenyon's attitude towards Michael annoyed me, I still sympathized with him. I imagined that he was getting flack from his superiors for not making progress in the case. Otilia had also mentioned that Michael wanted to hire a private agency to conduct a separate investigation. Joel's suicide hadn't appeased anyone's anger. If anything, it had opened up more questions than it had answered.

After closing the file folder, Kenyon put it down on his desk.

"Where do you go from here?" I asked him. "It seems to me you aren't any closer to finding little Michael's killer than you were last Saturday."

"You sound just like *him*." He took off his glasses and rubbed his eyes.

Knowing that Kenyon was referring to Michael Cisneros, I asked him. "Has *he* been giving you a hard time?"

Kenyon nodded by way of an answer. "He does have friends in high places, you know."

"Are you in trouble? I mean ... with the department?"

He shook his head. "Everything that can be done is being done. But this is a tough one, no doubt about it ... ."

After my encounter with Joel, I had at first intended to give Kenyon the photo fragments, but then decided to keep them, mostly to show them to Otilia. She hadn't recognized the strange emblem on the killer's pants, however. The other clue I had obtained had to do with the scar Mando had seen on the killer. I finally told Kenyon about this, explaining that Mando had believed that this scar was part of the killer's disguise. Kenyon had tilted his head and nodded, seemingly agreeing with Mando's interpretation.

"Maybe this will help, too." I handed Kenyon the envelope where I'd put the fragments of the photographs.

"Gloria, Gloria. You've been a naughty girl."

Since it hadn't been my intention to deceive him, I ignored his remark and gave him my ideas about the possible significance of the photos. "Before Joel fled from you on Monday," I reminded him, "he said that *they* had taken him to 'Rio,' and that *he* had made promises. I don't know about you, but I believe the people who hired him, including the main honcho, took him to Rio de Janeiro. And maybe these people in Rio are part of a group—a lodge, perhaps—that bears this as their emblem.

What do you think?"

Kenyon nodded while he looked at the fragments of the photos, using his reading glasses like a magnifying glass.

"Quite a strange looking symbol," he commented, examining the photo of the killer's back pants-pocket. "Hmmm. It's a human hand grasping a lion's paw. Above them is a circle—a crown—of fire. A cross seems to rise from the center of the circle. What do you think it means?"

"Neither Luisa nor Otilia nor I know what to make of it. I was hoping you'd be able to tell me.

"No, I can't, but maybe Professor Rivers at U.C.L.A., our geneology and heraldry expert, has come across this emblem or a similar one researching for his books."

"Lucky, we are," I said, frowning—but glad, in this case—that someone had actually pursued such an esoteric course of study.

"Amen!" Kenyon walked back to the window. Expecting to see something peculiar or important going on outside, I joined him. But I was wrong, for this was just another ordinary day in the parking lot of the L.A.P.D. Perhaps, for a cop whose days were numbered, an ordinary day was a most important event.

"Now that I'm leaving, will you at least tell me what they call this ... condition you have?"

Kenyon pointed at his temple, as if his index finger were the barrel of a gun. An aneurism or a brain tumor, he was saying. But whatever this disease was, it would take his life as surely as a gunshot through his brain.

After a quiet moment together, he said, "I suppose it wouldn't do any good to ask you to forget about all this." I only smiled in response.

A few minutes later, we began our race through the L.A. freeways, first to Luisa's apartment to pick up my belongings, then to the airport. After patiently standing in line with me while I waited to check in, Kenyon walked me to the boarding area. The other passengers had started to board. He shook my hand, and without saying a word, turned to leave.

"I'll call ... ," I started to say, but changed my mind. As I moved through the jetway, the pulsating light of Matthew Kenyon's star began to fade; by the time I reached my seat it was gone. Instead, I was aware that the next day, under a spruce or a magnolia tree overlooking the San Francisco Bay, Michael David would be lowered into the ground to dream the dreams of the dead.

The only way I could avoid thinking about the jet plunging into a deep abyss was to be oblivious to it. So after installing myself on my seat, I went to sleep. When I opened my eyes again, the flight attendant had dimmed the cabin lights. I looked out the window. Down below, the shimmering stream of automobile lights on the San Mateo-Hayward Bridge announced to my weary soul and mind the nearness of warm, loving arms. In the span of five days I had travelled a hundred years. On the plane's final approach, the lights in the cabin came back on. My reflection flashed briefly on the window. I looked away for fear I might see a century-old woman staring back at me.

Interlude

Who will it be?
And what will he say
When he arrives?
From the distance
He'll call out, "Butterfly."
Without answering, at first
I will stay away,
Partly to tease him,
Partly not to die
At our first encounter ...

From "Un bel di,"
Madame Butterfly
by Giacomo Puccini

FIFTEEN
Voices and Visions

Robbing Tania and Darío of my attention, and often going without sleep and nourishment, I gathered as much information as I could about the Cisneros and the Peralta families during the period of six months that followed my return to Oakland. Soon, I had a box full of business profiles of Black Swan Enterprises and gossip columns with photos of Michael and Lillian, and of Paul Cisneros at various social and cultural functions.

Afraid that I would forget something important, I set down on paper the day-to-day activities I'd had with Kenyon in Los Angeles, and kept a journal of every conceivable clue I had come across since the murders.

Relentlessly, I pursued any lead that might clarify the connection between the Peraltas, the Cisneros and Cecilia Castro-Biddle.

In early December, 1970, reading through the archives at the Oakland History Room, I discovered two items of interest. In 1957, a newspaper article mentioned that Cecilia Castro-Biddle's daughter lived in the Santa Cruz mountains. A few years later, another article referred to a small park that had been named after the Peraltas, and was located in the Fruitvale District, the heart of the Spanish-speaking community in Oakland. As soon as the weather permitted, I took Tania to play at my newly discovered Peralta Historical Park, and by felicitous coincidence, or so I thought at first, I met Charlotte and Celie Lamont, two elderly women who lived across from the park. Later I found out that chance had little to do with my meeting them, for they were often outside, even in winter, taking care of their garden and greeting everyone who visited the park.

Charlotte and Celie immediately took to Tania and me, and invited us to have some refreshments with them. Later, they asked us to pay them another visit. I liked them as well, and on several occasions I visited with them while Tania played in the park.

Charlotte was an opera enthusiast, and one day I found her listening to a recording of Puccini's *Madame Butterfly*. As the soprano began the first few phrases of the aria "Un bel di," I recognized the music that had been resonating in my head numerous times ever since the afternoon Luisa and I had come upon little Michael's body.

"What is this song we're hearing?" I asked Charlotte.

Instead of answering my question, she asked one of her own, "Do you know the story of Madame Butterfly?"

I didn't I said. Charlotte, always eager to talk about the librettoes of her favorite operas, was delighted with the prospect of telling me about Madame Butterfly.

"Pinkerton," Charlotte began, "is an American Navy officer stationed in Japan, who falls in love with Cio-Cio San, a Japanese lady; he decides to marry her in accordance with Japanese protocol. Endearingly he calls her Butterfly. Pinkerton is called back to the United States, but he promises Butterfly he'll be back for her. Pinkerton's marriage to Cio-Cio San is not valid in the States, however, and when he falls in love with another woman, Kate, he marries her. In the meantime, Cio-Cio San gives birth to a son and waits for Pinkerton to return. Three years pass by, apparently enough time to provide grounds for a divorce, Japanese style. Prince Yamadori asks Cio-Cio San to marry him, but she turns him down. Then Pinkerton returns to Japan with his new bride, and his best friend in Japan, Consul Sharpless, informs him about his son. Pinkerton decides to take his son back with him to the U.S. Realizing he never loved her, Butterfly commits hara-kiri.

"Poor Butterfly," Charlotte lamented. "She literally spilled her guts for a poor excuse of a man while all the time a perfectly decent Prince Yamadori was in love with her."

"I really like this aria," I commented.

"It's called 'Un bel di,' " Charlotte offered, then proceeded to tell me what the lyrics were about. "Butterfly is looking at the ocean, trying to imagine how things will be when Pinkerton's ship sails into the harbor. She imagines her joy at seeing him approach her house, calling out for her. She'll then come out to greet him, and they'll love each other with as much passion as on their first meeting." Charlotte wound up her explanation as Celie came into the room. Then Charlotte asked, "Why does this aria interest you, Gloria?"

Without going into my visions, I told the Lamont sisters about the murder of the child and how in my mind I connected this song with his mother. The more I told them, the more intrigued they became with my story. When I mentioned that I had been keeping a file on the case, they asked me if they could see some of the newspaper articles and the photos

I had saved.

The next day, I brought some of my files to show them. They looked first at the photos of the Cisneros brothers that had accompanied a business item about Black Swan Enterprises. Pointing to a photo of Paul, Celie said, "I've seen this man before. I'm almost sure Charlotte and I have met him."

Charlotte glanced at the photo over Celie's shoulder. "Yes. He does seem familiar. I am almost sure he is the handsome young man whose brother was kidnapped, then abandoned here, at the park, a few hours after he was abducted."

"Are you saying that the young man's brother was recently kidnapped?" I asked, unsure of what Charlotte meant.

"No. That's not what I'm saying. We met this young man here at the park in February of this year," Charlotte said pointing at Paul Cisneros' picture. "It was his brother back in nineteen forty-something, while he was still a child, who was kidnapped. Later he was found at *this* park. Don't you remember what this young man Paul told us, Celie? It was your favorite Peralta Park story and for days you couldn't stop talking about it. You must have told half of Oakland that story."

"Not half of Oakland, Charlotte," Celie responded with a smile. "But you're absolutely right. This is the man and his name *is* Paul." Celie then turned to me and noted, "Paul told us that the kidnapping happened back in 1941. That's long before we came to live in this house."

"Did he give you any details about his brother's kidnapping?" I asked them, then added, "That's something I know nothing about."

"Paul told us," Charlotte responded, "that his brother had been about four at the time of the kidnapping." Then, glancing at another newspaper photo, she asked, "Is the man in this other photo the brother who was kidnapped?"

"Michael," Celie reminded Charlotte. "Paul told us his brother's name is Michael."

"Yes," I confirmed. "The man in the other photo is Michael Cisneros, Paul's brother. But as I told you, I had no idea he'd been kidnapped."

"Paul must be the younger brother, don't you think?" Celie looked at her sister, who answered with a nod.

"Yes," I verified. "Paul is about four years younger than Michael, so he might not have been born when his brother was kidnapped. Did Paul tell you who it was that kidnapped Michael?"

"As I recall, I don't think anybody knew that. Paul did tell us that his mother said the kidnapper was a woman." Charlotte answered, then added, "But I remember Paul said that at the time of the kidnapping, his parents didn't contact the police."

Celie quickly interjected, "He said his parents didn't want a scandal, so they didn't tell anyone about it for a long time. From that, we assumed they didn't call the police."

"Why would a kidnapping cause a scandal for the Cisneros?" I exclaimed, unintentionally.

"We also asked the same question, but Paul didn't seem to know the reason. Or at least he didn't tell us," Celie responded.

"And you say Paul told you all this at the beginning of this year?" I asked, ascertaining the date again.

"It was late February. I know because we gave him a bunch of freshly cut daffodils. Remember? The daffodils always bloom in late February." Celie reminded Charlotte.

I went home all confused and intrigued with this turn of events. It was now early December in the year 1970, and Paul had talked to the Lamont Sisters in February, about six months before little Michael had been murdered in East L.A.

Later that day, after I put Tania to bed, I called Otilia in L.A. and asked her if she'd known that Michael Cisneros had been kidnapped when he was a child.

"All I know," Otilia said, "is that a maid saw a woman watching the house a couple of times on the day before Michael disappeared. She didn't make much of it until Michael was taken. But that was almost thirty years ago. I don't see what that has to do with my grandson's death." Otilia paused, then added, "We all appreciate what you and Luisa have done to help in the investigation, but not even Detective Kenyon ... What I'm trying to say, Gloria, is that maybe it is time for you ... for all of us to go on with our lives."

Wishing that I could put the case to rest, but knowing I wouldn't be able to do so, immediately after talking to Otilia, I phoned Luisa and asked her to relay this new information to Kenyon.

I was beginning to sense there was a connection between Michael's abduction and little Michael's murder. I felt more and more certain that somehow the woman called Cecilia Castro-Biddle was responsible for Michael's abduction. Could she possibly also have taken little Michael David from Otilia's house? Was she an accessory to the murder? Had I been wrong all along in assuming that the murderer was a man rather than a woman?

The columnist who had written about Mrs. Castro-Biddle's family back in 1957 had mentioned that Cecilia's daughter lived in the Santa Cruz Mountains, but she hadn't given any information about the woman's name, her age or marital status, not even her city of residence. Knowing that Los Gatos and Saratoga were the two important cities in that mountain region, I made a trip to the area. A brief inquiry at the local library and newspaper office proved fruitless. Fortunately, as I was walking out of the office, it occurred to me that the Castro-Biddles might be Catholics. My hunch paid off when I again spoke with the receptionist at the newspaper office.

A Mexican-American family who lived in the mountains where the homes had several acres of woods around them, would probably worship at the Sacred Heart Church, just north of the Los Gatos-Saratoga area, the receptionist told me. People in more modest areas would most likely attend services in San Jose.

Despite my dislike for judging offspring in accordance with their parents' social preferences, in this case I had to consider that Mrs. Castro-Biddle's daughter, like her mother, would never worship with the likes of farmworkers and waiters. So I headed for the Church of the Sacred Heart, which was in the most affluent part of town.

Father John Stewart, the parish priest, was in his early sixties. He had small bright eyes and a mischievous smile that made him look as if he were about to tell a joke or laugh at one.

"I'm trying to locate a Mrs. Cecilia Castro-Biddle. I thought that she might be one of your parishioners."

Father Stewart studied my face for a few seconds, then said: "Yes, I know the family well. I've been their confessor for many years." He paused, then added, "Cecilia—Mrs. Castro-Biddle—has been dead for about four months."

The instant I heard the news I felt a gust of air coming out of my lungs, as if someone had punched me in the stomach.

The Father continued, saying, "She took her own life. She swallowed a bottleful of pills. May God have mercy on her soul."

"Amen," I said, and as a sign of respect I waited for a minute or so before I went on with my inquiry. "Did she ever mention the Cisneros family of Oakland to you?"

Father Stewart didn't answer my question, which indicated to me I might be on to something important, but I could tell he wasn't going to help me. Perhaps he couldn't. Even if she was dead, he was not going to betray any secret Cecilia Castro-Biddle might have told him.

"I have reason to believe that the motive for the murder of a youngster in Los Angeles, a little boy named Michael David Cisneros, had some connection to Mrs. Castro-Biddle. Somehow she was related to the Cisneros family and the Peralta family," I said but, as I expected, Father

Stewart offered no comments. Trying to find a way to obtain his help, I proposed an alternative. "I know that you can't betray her confidence, but I was hoping you would be able to give me information not told to you in confession about the family."

He considered my proposal for a few seconds, and finally said, "Yes, I might be able to do that."

Under the circumstances, I decided to tell him what I'd been able to piece together about Cecilia's identity, hoping he could add to that information. I began by telling him details about the genealogy of the Peralta family, beginning with the patriarch, Luis Peralta. Of his seventeen children, only five of them survived into adulthood and had families of their own. Luis Peralta had moved to San Jose with his only living daughter and had distributed the rest of the land among his four surviving sons. Vicente Peralta—the man whom Cecilia Castro-Biddle claimed as her direct ancestor—had received the Rancho San Antonio as legacy. This Rancho had spread over the entire area that was now the city of Oakland, across the bay from San Francisco.

Vicente Peralta played an important role in the politics of the region, for while the territory was still under Mexican rule, Vallejo had been governor of California, and Peralta had been not only Vallejo's good friend but also a general in the Mexican army. On July 10, 1846, during the Bear Flag Revolt, rebels fought and defeated Vallejo's army, with the intention of taking California away from Mexican rule. As a result, General Vallejo, his brother, and Vicente Peralta had been imprisoned at Sutter's Fort, but were later released. In 1848, California was annexed by the United States. About that time, gold was discovered and squatters had begun to occupy more and more of Peralta's land. At the time of his death in June of 1871, Peralta had recently sold what remained of his Rancho San Antonio. Peralta's wife, Encarnación, and their only daughter, Guadalupe, were thought to be his sole immediate survivors.

"But I know Mrs. Castro-Biddle claimed to be a descendant of Vicente Peralta on her mother's side," I continued. "As far as I know, Peralta had the one daughter, Guadalupe. Cecilia cannot be Guadalupe's daughter because everyone on that side is accounted for. But in the documents I read at the library I came across the possibility that Vicente Peralta might have had another daughter, most likely an adopted one. So I'm assuming that Mrs. Castro-Biddle's right to the Peralta name was through the line of the adopted daughter of whom not much is known."

"Yes," Father Stewart said. "That's right so far. This adopted daughter of the Peraltas, whose name Cecilia told me was Josefa Asunción, went to live in Mexico, in Cuernavaca. There she met and married

Ernesto Castro Carriles and had three children—two sons, Manuel and Eladio, and a daughter, Cecilia. Our Cecilia Castro-Biddle."

"So, did Cecilia live in Cuernavaca most of her life?"

"No. Cecilia's father was from a socially prominent family in Mexico, but wanted his children to keep their right to their U.S. citizenship, to which they were entitled since their mother was an American citizen. So he sent them to school in the States. Then part of the family moved to the Bay Area. Cecilia was at Mills College in Oakland, as a matter of fact, until she ran away. No one knew where she was, but eventually she was found in Mexico City."

"What had she been doing there?"

Father Stewart smiled, but didn't say anything.

"Was she all right when she came back to the States?" I pressed on.

"Not quite. It might have been the onset of her emotional condition ..."

"That ended when she committed suicide," I completed his statement.

He smiled and looked at me as if asking, "Why are you interested in all this, Gloria?" but he didn't say anything.

"One last question, Father. When was Cecilia a student at Mills?"

The priest's eyes showed hesitation as he weighed the ethical questions before answering me. Realizing the information was a matter of record at the college, he said, "It was during the mid-thirties. 1936 was the year she disappeared."

My heart leaped inside my chest. "Thank you," I said to Father Stewart.

"Glad to be of help, my daughter. I pray I didn't place a cross on your shoulders."

"None that wasn't there before, Father."

On my way back to Oakland, I kept reviewing the information I had just heard and some of the pieces began to fall into place. Michael Cisneros Jr. had been born in Mexico City in 1937, the same year that Cecilia had lived in that city anonymously. I surmised that, afraid that her parents would find out she was pregnant out of wedlock, she had arranged privately for the Cisneros to adopt her child—not an uncommon practice then. But, had she changed her mind about giving up her son? And four years later, had she taken Michael from the Cisneros' house? Still afraid of her parents' rejection or perhaps already emotionally unbalanced, had Cecilia then left Michael at the Peralta Historical Park?

At the time, Karen and Michael Cisneros Sr. had not notified the police about their son's disappearance because they feared a "scandal." The "scandal" was probably connected to the adoption. Perhaps in 1941, people were not so open about adoptions for fear the adopted child would be jeered at or humiliated by other children around him. Or perhaps the Cisneros, as a wealthy couple, were already concerned with their son's inheritance.

Since the first time I saw Michael and Lillian's wedding photos, I had been aware that Michael Jr. was physically very different from the rest of the Cisneros. As unpredictable as the laws of heredity might be, it was obvious that Michael was quite the opposite of his brother Paul, and so unlike his mother and father that one wouldn't have connected him to that family if one had met them separately. I wondered if Michael had ever been told that he was adopted. Did Lillian and Otilia know about it? Could it be that Paul was also adopted?

The revelation that Michael might be Cecilia Castro-Biddle's child offered no solution to the mystery. It simply brought into view a new set of questions. In what way was this information relevant to the case, I asked myself.

As soon as I got home I headed for the telephone, but I suddenly decided not to dial Kenyon's number. Since I had unsuccessfully attempted to talk to him at the L.A.P.D. on numerous occasions, Darío had already raised mild objections to my calling long-distance so often. Instead of trying to reach Kenyon by phone, I wrote him a long letter, explaining about Michael's kidnapping, his possible adoption and Mrs. Castro-Biddle's alleged role in both situations. I also sent copies of all my files to his office in L.A.

Unable to cope with the frustration, I often called Luisa hoping that she had heard from Kenyon or Otilia about any new developments in the case. But Luisa never heard from Kenyon again and, politely but firmly, Otilia refused to discuss the subject.

Deep down, I knew I was becoming obsessed with the case, but I was already too involved to heed my own warnings.

SIXTEEN

The Dead Also Whisper

On January 2, 1971, shortly after three o'clock in the morning, I woke from a deep sleep for no apparent reason. For a few seconds I was conscious of a throbbing pain in the front of my head. When I got up that morning my pillow was moist and my eyes hurt. That afternoon when I picked up Tania at her school, I had a message from my mother, asking me to stop by her house. Luisa had called, confirming what I'd been trying to ignore all day long: Matthew Kenyon had died in the early hours of the morning. Since he had been unable to locate Reyna Galeano or make any progress in the case, the murder of Michael David Cisneros was being filed in the archives of the unsolved crimes section.

During the next few days, I thought about nothing but Kenyon. I felt devastated. Aware that my sorrow was probably little compared to Mrs. Kenyon's grief, I immediately wrote to her. Not wanting to send my note of condolence to her at the police department, I asked Luisa to find out for me where I could write to the Kenyon family directly. The next day, Luisa phoned to tell me that she had obtained the Kenyons' address in Santa Barbara, but suggested I send my note to her instead. Since she was planning to visit Mrs. Kenyon, she could deliver my message personally.

In a few days, Luisa wrote, informing me that she had been to Santa Barbara and that a letter from Annie Kenyon would soon follow. To my surprise and delight, two weeks later, instead of a letter, a package from Kenyon's widow arrived. Suspecting that it contained Matthew Kenyon's personal file on the case, I tore open the accompanying envelope immediately and read Annie Kenyon's cover letter:

> "I am sending you copies of every report and piece of information that my husband was able to gather about the death of Michael David Cisneros. This was one of two cases in his whole career where he was completely at a loss. Matt

was very fond of you and spoke about you often, but felt he had put you in enough danger already, so he never sent these records. I know he would have liked for you to have them. Best of luck and warm regards."

Annie Kenyon.

Kenyon's file contained several very important pieces of information. The first one was the coroner's analyses of little Michael's blood and of the excrement in his mouth. The feces contained traces of coconut oil, bits of crayfish, and tropical fruit enzymes. All of this information was of little help since bananas, papayas, pineapples and other tropical fruits were easily bought in any U.S. supermarket.

The second report was the chemical analysis of little Michael's blood. It contained a formula I didn't even attempt to read, and lots of handwritten notes by a forensics expert on an alkaloid extracted from the Pereira bark—*Pereirine*—an extremely uncommon element in North America. The bark was from a plant natural to Brazil, used in the form of a tonic for medicinal purpose, mostly as a febrifuge, to bring down fever.

The report also stated that little is known about the uses of Pereira bark in folk medicine, but apparently the extract when mixed with sugar cane brandy has an effect on sexual performance, like an aphrodisiac, I guessed. On the other hand, a French botanist claimed that this alkaloid might have some of the characteristics of the *curare*, also found in the Amazon jungle, and often used by the region's tribesmen to paralyze their prey.

Of particular interest in Kenyon's file was the classification of the insignia found on the man who had carried little Michael's body to Marigold Street. This emblem had been traced through the fragments of photos I'd found in Joel Galeano's fireplace by Professor Rivers of U.C.L.A., who had reported that the emblem was only a fragment of a larger insignia which had been used by a Brazilian brotherhood in the early part of the century. Some of the motifs indicated that the larger emblem might be of German-Austrian origin.

I was hardly able to contain my enthusiasm, as I realized that the existence of a Brazilian brotherhood fit in with what Joel Galeano had said about the people who had taken him to Rio de Janeiro. He had also mentioned that someone who was a member of this group had given him a great deal of money.

As far as I knew, the Cisneros had no business interests in Brazil, but for some time already, Black Swan had been growing and diversifying at a rapid rate.

I reviewed the information I had collected about the Cisneros' company. For at least two decades, under Michael Sr.'s direction, the business had maintained a solid financial base and sound reputation. The family owned several hardware stores in Northern California, in addition to the construction company.

Then, in the early fifties, with a boom in housing development, Black Swan had experienced enormous growth and the company had acquired two cement plants.

I had also found out that in 1956, an already renowned industrialist, Soren Bjorgun, Karen Cisneros' father, had become a partner in the company. His investment had made it possible for Michael Sr. to acquire two steel mills in Oakland, where tools and metal sheeting for airplanes and ships were manufactured.

Intrigued, I mulled over the possible reasons why a few years later, for undisclosed reasons, Soren Bjorgun left Black Swan, transferring his twenty-five-percent ownership of the company to his grandson, Paul Cisneros, for his eighteenth birthday. Rumors claimed that there had been a falling out between the two partners, but as far as I could tell, the company had remained stable for many years. About that time, Karen Cisneros died of kidney failure, leaving her shares in the company to her son Michael.

When Michael Sr.'s health worsened, Michael Jr. took over the company, then became its president and the principal stockholder after his father died in 1967. He changed the name of the company to Black Swan International Enterprises, and there were rumors in financial circles that Michael Jr. intended to have Black Swan become a public corporation, in order to attract international investors but that hadn't happened; so far, Black Swan had remained a family-owned enterprise.

Not knowing enough about sound business decisions, I could judge Michael's performance only by the success of his company's expansion program. As part of his plan, Black Swan had sold a lumber mill, one of the cement plants, and all the hardware stores. The funds were reinvested in two larger steel mills in the Bay Area, and in equipping a plant to begin manufacturing fiberboards and fiberoptics.

The Cisneros brothers were in the process of creating a market for both their soft and hard products abroad as well. In particular, Paul Cisneros was in charge of establishing the necessary contacts and negotiations with several companies in other countries.

At the time of little Michael's murder, Paul had been in Germany on company business. I wondered if Brazil was also one of those nations being courted by the Cisneros' company. Might there be a connection between the Brazilian brotherhood and Black Swan?

Voicing my concerns to Luisa about the possibility, I then agreed to let her contact Kenyon's partner, McGuire, at the L.A.P.D. A few days later, she phoned back. McGuire had told her that back in October he had gotten in touch with Interpol because of similar suspicions Kenyon had. Although the international cops didn't deny that such a secret society might exist, they had no actual proof of any brotherhood operating in Brazil as of then.

Determined to help me with the investigation, Luisa made an unsuccessful attempt to locate Reyna Galeano through her mother, Sylvia Castañeda, who still lived in Santa Monica. Although she didn't directly ask Sylvia for her daughter's address, Luisa had hoped somehow to come across the information during one of her visits. But she never gained even a hint from Sylvia as to Reyna's whereabouts.

Then, towards the end of 1971, about a year after Reyna had disappeared, her mother also went away unexpectedly. Again, hoping to find out Mrs. Castañeda's new address, Luisa paid a visit to Sylvia's neighbor and good friend, Betsy Hinkle. Even though Mrs. Hinkle lead Luisa to believe she knew where both Reyna and Sylvia were living, she did not disclose their address. Disheartened, Luisa called to tell me that she was giving up her search.

That day, as I was talking to her, I began to notice a slight tremor in my hands that continued throughout the afternoon. I managed to keep Darío from noticing the trembling. But after dinner, as I was loading the dishwasher, my heart began to race. Shaking violently I broke a glass I was holding. Vaguely, I remember feeling lightheaded and seeing blood all over the sink.

Hearing the sound of broken glass, Darío called out, and when I didn't respond, he rushed to the kitchen, where he found me holding on to the edge of the sink with bloody hands. I kept saying over and over, "I won't die. I won't die." As he forced me to loosen my grip on the sink, I passed out. Later, as if in a dream, I heard him whisper in my ear, "Please, Gloria. You can't go on like this. You're killing yourself. Think of Tania—she needs you. I need you too."

At Darío's insistance, I spent the next twenty-four hours at the hospital. There I was hooked to an IV feeding tube and given a series of tests. Then I spent a week in bed at home, unable to use my bandaged hands. My mother and my husband spoonfed me.

When I began to regain my strength, I started looking for my files on little Michael's murder, but I couldn't find them anywhere. My mother, under repeated interrogation, finally confessed that Darío had taken the box the day I'd come home from the hospital. She had no idea where he'd put it.

During all the years we had been married, Darío and I had managed to avoid major arguments. So, afraid we would now get into a heated discussion, I decided to wait for an appropriate opportunity to ask him for my files. The day the lab sent back my test results, indicating that I suffered from nothing more than anemia and over-all exhaustion, my husband was in a good mood. Much to my surprise, on his own, he went to his office and came back with my box.

"I know I shouldn't have gone through your papers," he said, "but I needed to find out what it was you were risking your health and happiness for."

"That's fine. I'm just glad to have my files back," I said, trying to keep calm.

I was very aware that I had never mentioned to him my brush with death at Joel Galeano's house, and as I expected, Darío gave me a long look, then said, "You never told me that you were held at gunpoint. What has happened to you, Gloria? Is tinkering with this case so important to you that you would risk everything for it?" More than angry or worried, Darío's voice betrayed his disappointment in me.

"I've never told you what to do," he went on without giving me a chance to offer an explanation. "And I *never* kept you from doing what you thought was best. But you've never been reckless before. Now you're endangering your life, with no regard for Tania's well-being or mine." He paused, trying to contain his feelings, waiting for my reaction. What could I say? Denying or making up excuses for my behavior would get me nowhere. I kept quiet.

"I will not keep you from going on with your investigation," he continued. "These extrasensory experiences of yours are obviously more important to you than your own safety." Darío was clearly issuing me a challenge as he stated, "But think about this. What is more important for you, solving this case or keeping our marriage and family together? That is something *you* alone will have to decide." Then, he walked out of the room.

I drove to the cemetery overlooking the bay. There, I mulled over Darío's words for hours. Sitting by Michael David's grave, I kept going over my silent promise to him and to Mando: that I would help bring to justice whomever was responsible for their deaths. But, I also struggled with the fact that years before, I had promised my daughter on the day she was born that her well-being would be foremost in my life. I also knew that, without Darío, my life was simply inconceivable. So I reluctantly went home, packed up and sealed my file box, closing the book on Michael David's murder.

Throughout our years together, I had no reason to regret my decision, for Darío remained a loving and understanding husband and father, and my daughter brought nothing but joy into my life.

As far as everyone was concerned, I had left behind that part of my life, but secretly I still cut out and saved news about the Cisneros. During all that time, I also maintained a friendship with Otilia Juárez and visited her at Lillian and Michael Cisneros' house when she came to visit them in Oakland. On occasions, Darío even took Otilia and me out to dinner, for he also seemed to enjoy her company.

Although I never again discussed the case with anyone except Luisa, my visions still came to me every so often. Sometimes in the middle of the night, I'd wake up to a soprano's voice singing the aria "Un bel di," sounding so clear and near that I swore the singer was in the house. Whenever this happened, just before I opened my eyes, Lillian's face would flash in my memory, and a hand wearing a ring with a lion's head would reach out and wrap around her neck.

SEVENTEEN

Vineyards and Graveyards

At age twenty-three I had first confronted this other self, this psychic being who insisted on my relinquishing control of a part of my life to . . . to an automatic pilot. Like someone who has been told she's terminally ill, I went through two years of denial, then worked slowly towards knowing what ailed me. Eventually, I learned to accept this dark gift and to build the delicate balance on which my sanity rested.

Over the years, I had many of these "prophetic" dreams and visions in connection with little Michael's murder. Their meaning always eluded me. But one of those premonitions in particular intrigued me. I asked myself why, sometimes yielding to some inexplicable urgency, I drove to the corner of Monterey and Leimert in the foothills of Oakland. What was to happen at that corner? I knew that although there was no house at that spot now, a charming residence belonging to the Cisneros had once stood there and that Lillian and Michael had been living in that house when little Michael was killed. Then, in 1975, the house on Monterey and Leimert had burned down while the Cisneros were on holiday in Greece. Dispelling the rumors of possible arson, the fire inspectors said the blaze had been the result of a short in an appliance. Michael and Lillian had not rebuilt the house, moving instead to Snake Road in the Oakland hills.

Then, in 1980, an item in the business section of the Oakland newspaper announced the acquisition by Michael Cisneros of Solera, a small winery just outside the town of Saint Helena, in the Napa Valley. It seemed odd that Michael would purchase such a business. Later, Lillian's mother Otilia told me that the business was not very profitable for Michael, but that he kept it to please Lillian, who preferred to live at Solera. From then on, it seemed that the Cisneros went back and forth between Saint Helena and Oakland.

In the summer of 1984, Luisa moved back to Oakland, and while

Darío took Tania to visit his parents in New York, Luisa and I went up to Solera to see Otilia, who was spending a few weeks with Lillian. On the day of our visit, Lillian and Michael were in San Francisco at a fund-raiser for the opera. Otilia took us on a tour of the winery grounds. Surrounded by the vineyards, the house was a U-shaped structure, with the rooms opening onto a spacious hall, running the length of the house. A courtyard separated the residence from the winery, the office, and the sales and tasting rooms. Rows of roses served as a fence to a patio with picnic tables and a gazebo.

In the course of our visit, Paul Cisneros drove up to pick up some business papers he needed. He was a suave, very handsome and sociable man. When Otilia introduced us to him, Luisa kept staring at Paul, who seemed amused rather than annoyed by Luisa's attention. Although he'd been romantically linked to a number of socially-prominent women, and in the last few years he had kept steady company with Cynthia Sarks, heiress to a California chain of jewelry stores, Paul didn't seem to be in any hurry to marry anyone.

"I thought you and Cynthia would be at the fund-raiser," Otilia had commented.

"Cynthia is visiting her grandmother in North Carolina. And I'm leaving for Stockholm tomorrow. I have quite a few things to take care of before I leave in the early morning."

"Business or pleasure?" Otilia asked.

"Business," Paul replied. "This time, I'll be doing business with some of Grandfather's relatives in the old country. I haven't seen them in many years—actually not since Grandfather's funeral."

"You still miss your grandfather a whole lot?"

"Of course," Paul said, as he let his gaze slide down the rows of vineyards extending in perfect geometrical alignment. Then, he murmured something I couldn't hear. Luisa, sitting closer to him, told me later that he had referred to the vineyards as "the tombstones of Saint Helena." Aloud, Paul had commented, "This place is quite idyllic. Michael and Lillian are such a pair of romantics." He turned around to look at Otilia, then added, "I hope they never lose Solera."

Since I hadn't made him the object of my admiration, he gave me only a passing glance at first. Later on, our eyes met a few times when I began to look at him attentively though not directly. This seemed to make him uneasy, for soon after, he got up to leave. Paul seemed to be used to women looking admiringly at him, but he was obviously uncomfortable when he felt observed.

"Michael's always telling me Paul is such a romantic," Otilia said, af-

ter Paul had left. "And just a while ago, Paul called Michael a romantic."
She laughed.

"What makes Michael say that Paul's a romantic?" I asked, "He
strikes me as a lonely man, but a *romantic*? I don't know about that."

"Well, I'm inclined to believe Michael," Otilia began. "I'll tell you
why. One of those times I was visiting Lilly in Oakland, we were invited
to Paul's house in San Francisco. He had thrown a big party to commem-
orate the anniversary of his mother's birthday, which he combined with
a Christmas celebration. There was a houseful of guests, so it seemed
strange to see Paul in his study going through a box that belonged to his
late father. I stopped at the door and made some silly remark about his
going through 'old memories.' At first he gave me a vacant look, but
when he really looked at me, I could see that he was angry. I apologized
and joined the rest of the guests in the living room. Later, I mentioned
the incident to Michael, mostly because I felt embarrassed. After all, I
didn't want either one of them to think that I was being nosy or that I'd
been spying on Paul."

"What was Michael's response?"

"He laughed and told me not to worry," Otilia answered. "Michael
said that Paul was always going through boxes—his treasure boxes—and
that Paul loved to collect stuff—photos, notes, other little mementos, toys
he and Michael had gotten on various birthdays, odds and ends. That's
when Michael called his brother a 'romantic,' but warned me that Paul
feels very protective of his intimate treasures."

"So, what did he keep in the box?" I asked.

"His father's personal papers, I suppose. Michael was very busy
trying to keep the business going after Michael Sr. died. Since their
mother had died by then, Paul had to take care of his father's personal
affairs."

"I gather Paul was very close to his mother," Luisa said, and added,
"Was he her favorite?"

"I don't think Karen preferred one son over the other. But, at the risk
of being wrong, I think she and Michael seemed to have more things in
common." Otilia paused. "On the other hand," she continued, "Paul told
me that he always felt closer to his grandfather Bjorgun. He also said that
he felt as if he were an orphan when his grandfather died." Otilia paused
again, then she offered, "His grandfather died only a few weeks after he
had a bitter argument with Michael Sr. Every time I've heard either Paul
or Michael recount the argument, I've somehow gotten the impression
that for a time after his grandfather died, Paul blamed his father for old
man Bjorgun's death."

"What did the two men argue about?" Luisa asked.

"Apparently, old man Bjorgun wanted Michael Sr. to make Paul his assistant. I'm guessing when I say this, but I think that he never really cared much for either Michael Sr. or Michael Jr. I know that he was opposed to Karen's marriage to Michael Sr., but there was little he could do except threaten to disinherit his daughter. His threat didn't do him any good because Karen married Michael Sr. anyway."

"That's very interesting," I commented. "Because it was Soren Bjorgun who made it possible for Michael Sr. to expand his business."

"Of course," Otilia observed. "What better way to control someone than to own part of what he has!" She chuckled, a bit embarrassed at her outburst. "By now you've guessed I didn't think very highly of old man Bjorgun—though I must confess it's all gratuitous because I never even met the gentleman. But I've been told time and again about him, and he sounds to me like an extremely possessive man. Michael has also told me that his grandfather's only son, his uncle Frederik, went off to war, trying to get away from his father. Frederik died in the war, and the father became even more possessive of his daughter Karen. Who knows? But perhaps because Paul resembled Karen, the old man also tried to gain control over his grandson's life. Unfortunately, circumstances in Karen's life made it possible for Soren to do just that.

"When Paul was born, Karen developed acute nephritis, and her condition became so debilitating that she couldn't care for her new-born baby. Michael Sr. hired a nurse, but Mr. Bjorgun accused the nurse of neglecting Paul, and was able to convince Karen that his grandson would be better off in his and Mrs. Bjorgun's care. So, during the first four years of his life and every summer from then on, Paul lived with the Bjorguns.

"On several occasions the old man accused Karen of not loving Paul, of favoring Michael Jr. Then Karen tried to convince her father that wasn't so. And when she couldn't make him believe that Michael had done nothing to deserve his grandfather's rejection, she began to protect Michael more and more."

"What did Michael Sr. have to say about all that?" I asked.

"He was, of course, upset at having the Bjorguns take baby Paul, but he didn't want to create problems for his ailing wife. So, he simply accepted her decision and kept out of the whole affair. Unfortunately, he also stayed out of Paul's life for too long. By the time family life went back to normal, I think Paul had begun to listen to his grandfather Bjorgun and to pretty much disregard what his father said," Otilia noted as she wound up her story.

"Well," Luisa commented, "At least the family quarrels didn't cause a rift between the brothers." We all nodded.

At that moment, I became aware that my opinion of Paul had been dictated by someone else's idea of who he was—mostly social columnists and other reporters covering financial news. Up to now, I had not known any of the personal details of his life.

Seeing him looking at the vineyards, I had sensed his great loneliness and his melancholy, and I realized that Paul had learned to hide his true feelings and his vulnerability under layers of charm, wit and social correctness.

"Imagine," I told Luisa, as we were driving home, "I know it's idiotic to feel pity for someone who has everything anyone could ever want, but still I couldn't help feeling sorry for Paul."

"I understand," Luisa said. "There's something about him ... a kind of ... "

"Vulnerability," I offered.

"That's a good way of putting it," Luisa said. "I wonder why he has never gotten married?"

"Funny. I was thinking about that, too."

"You know, Gloria, back at Solera you had the perfect opportunity to ask Otilia about Michael's adoption. It seemed obvious to me that the grandfather, 'old man Bjorgun,' as Otilia calls him, knew that Michael was adopted and that's why he rejected his grandson."

There was a basis for Luisa's opinion, but I kept quiet, not wanting to open up the subject of the investigation for discussion.

After a brief pause, Luisa asked, "Do you think Darío would get terribly upset if you broke your promise to him?" I looked at her not really understanding what she meant. "I'm referring to your promise," she clarified, "to never continue with your investigation of little Michael's murder."

"I'm not going to put that to a test, not while Darío is alive," I stated categorically. "Besides," I added, "too much time has already passed. Where would I begin again? But, why do you ask?"

"I don't know. Lately, I've been thinking a lot about death and today, looking at Otilia, I realized that what brought us together with her and the Cisneros was little Michael's death." She smiled and shrugged her shoulders. "I guess I'm just being morbid. I'd like to find out who killed little Michael before I die."

"Sorry to disappoint you. I'm done with death for now," I stated.

How wrong I had been.

In the summer of 1986, while he and Darío were jogging, my father, who hadn't been sick a day in his life, collapsed and died shortly thereafter.

Ever since I had looked into the barrel of Joel Galeano's gun, I had learned to live with the possibility of getting killed. Then, when Kenyon had died, I had been too young to fully understand that dying as a natural conclusion of life was different from being *killed*. In the case of my father, in spite of my sorrow, I was able to accept his dying as a natural end to his life. I had even felt that in trying to understand the inevitability of his death, I had come to grips with my own mortality. But that was only an illusion, for nothing could prepare me for what was yet to come.

Unlike the expected arrival of the season, on the third day of spring in 1988, Darío died suddenly of a heart attack. The shock was so great that the days after his death still remain a blank for me. What hurt most was that I had said goodbye to my husband that morning with the absolute certainty he would be back in the evening, that we would listen to his favorite music while I helped him prepare dinner. But Darío's heart had other plans.

I knew then that I wasn't ready to take one more loss, one more farewell. The anger that Darío's death aroused raced aimlessly through me like a deranged bull in a ring, locking horns with the wind.

Why had he, a physician, let himself die? Why had *I* let him die? I, who had this extrasensory power, who had even tried to cultivate it during all these years, I hadn't been able to predict, let alone prevent, my husband's death. How unfair it seemed to be the recipient of a dark gift, yet to have it be so small and limited. All that I could ever hope for was to struggle along with the little talent I had. Only one thing seemed certain at the time, that no matter how limited this psychic gift was, it would remain a part of me until the day I died.

Trying to be brave and to not give into sorrow or self-pity, during the past few months I've insisted on going on with my life as normally as possible. But recently, I realized I couldn't sleep in the same bed Darío and I had shared for twenty-two years without having death dreams. One of them was a recurring nightmare in which I'd see Lillian and Otilia crying by my graveside, with my bloody clothes strewn around it. During the dream, and for hours afterwards, I had the strangest feeling that only a part of me was buried there as if I had been cut up into pieces and only a few of them had been found.

For endless weeks I walked around with a sorrow and a despondency that finally became a quiet, self-consuming despair. No longer able to concentrate on my work at the speech center, where I've been employed since September, 1970, I took an indefinite leave of absence.

One night as I cleared Darío's closet, I came across the box that contained the files I had assembled since the time of Michael David's murder. I spent the next week piecing together all the information I had gathered over eighteen years. As I wrote down my impressions, I felt myself starting to come alive again. Not bound any more by my promise to Darío nor by Tania's needs since she is already at the university and pretty much responsible for her own life. I've decided to resume my investigation of the case.

At first, I felt compelled to go through with it, primarily so I could finally fulfill my promise to Mando and to little Michael David. I wanted to be done with that part of my life. But as I became involved in the case again, I realized that I also wanted to experience once more the excitement and all those other powerful feelings that, eighteen years before, had made me look foward to each day with such anticipation.

Again, I began to walk around with a torrent of facts and dates, names and places connected with little Michael's murder buzzing persistently in my head. At the same time, my visions and dreams increased and changed in nature.

Often now, while I am awake, the luminous lyrics of "Un bel di" gather in my memory and Lillian Cisneros' full face, tears streaming down her cheeks, stares at me. She speaks Madame Butterfly's words and I feel her pain, like a thin glass blade piercing my head from front to back. I cry with her. I have appropriated her pain and with it comes the knowledge that she holds the key to her son's murder. A hand wearing a ring with a lion's head ring reaches out and wraps around her neck, only it isn't really her neck. It's mine. I can't free myself from its icy grip.

Each day, I become more convinced that Lillian is in danger. The last few times we have talked, Otilia has hinted that her daughter's mental balance has become more precarious with each passing hour. Lillian is now under psychiatric care.

Neither Michael nor Otilia, who for all practical purposes has moved in with the Cisneros, can figure out what is wrong with her or how to help her. Michael is so concerned about his wife that he has taken an indefinite leave of absence as the president of the company, remaining active only as the chairman of the board.

Paul has been acting as Black Swan's interim president. To add to the Cisneros' troubles, two weeks ago, an article in the paper mentioned that Black Swan seems to be experiencing financial difficulties. At the same time, Anaconda Sur International, one of the largest metallurgy and fiberoptics conglomerates, with headquarters in Frankfurt and holdings in Sweden, Brazil and South Africa, has proposed a *merger*, a takeover in reality, with Black Swan.

Instinctively, I know that all these seemingly unrelated events have a special significance, that something is stirring and that all of this is connected to the murder of Lillian's and Michael's son. I know that much. What I don't seem to have learned in all these years is how to keep secrets from my mother. Recently, I have begun to see the furrows on her forehead deepen as she observes me and tries to find out what it is that I am doing.

This time, I've decided I will do this alone, keeping to myself as much as possible to avoid my mother's detection. I will also try to not involve Luisa who has been going through a difficult time in her life. Her difficulties don't seem to be anything more than a normal case of midlife blues, aggravated by a serious injury to her wrist. But I think the last thing in the world my friend needs is to go gallavanting all over creation with me.

Three days ago, I went to Los Angeles. I looked up Betsy Hinkle, Sylvia Castañeda's old friend and neighbor in Santa Monica. I never dreamed that Mrs. Hinkle had kept in touch with Sylvia and Reyna during all this time. I suppose that after such a lapse, Mrs. Hinkle felt there was no harm in my contacting her friends. Quite readily, she gave me their address in Marysville, a town northeast of Oakland. By felicitous coincidence, Mrs. Hinkle also asked me to deliver to Reyna and Sylvia the Christmas presents she had intended to send by mail. I gladly agreed to play Santa for her.

Not having been to East L.A. since the Moratorium march in 1970, I decided to drive through the old barrio. As expected it has changed in some ways. In other instances, it seems as if things have stood still. Except for the fact that the Silver Dollar Cafe is now only a bar, and a plaque with Rubén Salazar's name is displayed somewhere around Laguna Park, there is little to remind people of the events that at the time we thought would shape our political future in California.

Perhaps, like everyone else, I had expected too much, I thought as I glanced over the walls along and around Whittier Boulevard. I looked for the familiar skull of the Santos gang; that, too, has been wiped from barrio walls. Instead, sprayed with metallic silver paint, the words "Stoners Now" appear every so often.

When I asked a record shop owner who these Stoners were, he said, "They're our new *home crop*. They're into heavy metal music and drugs; they worship Satan; and they hate the sound of Spanish. These guys are all young—none over seventeen," he continued. "Pray they never cross your path."

Disappointed with our socio-political gains and losses in Los Angeles, I started back to the Bay Area that very same day.

As soon as I was home, I knew something had changed around me. For days afterwards, I sensed whirls of blue light around bushes, shimmering in the distance and pursuing me in my dreams as I became aware that someone was following me.

When my mother announced she had hired a private detective to protect me, I was upset with her. But when I looked into Justin Escobar's eyes as he stared at me through the misty car window, I knew that the solution to this mystery was finally at hand.

1988

PART TWO

I come from a culture
that has a healthy respect for the sun
and worships death
as much as it loves flowers:
but the memory of that brown child
eighteen years dead
calls from the misty foothills
still,
his murder unavenged
his empty gaze, a tear in the weaving
of my days.

                              Luisa Cortez

EIGHTEEN

Before the Light

Unaware of the dramatic events about to unfold, Gloria had just finished telling Justin the story of little Michael's and Mando's murders. He had been so quiet that had she been asked to identify him by his voice, at that moment, she would not have been able to do so. But she would recognize him anywhere by his curly hair, his oval face, his small bright eyes and well-shaped mouth.

Breaking the long pause, Justin finally asked Gloria, "What are your plans now?"

"I've asked Otilia to have lunch with me tomorrow. I intend to tell her everything I know and ask for her help. Then I'll go up to Marysville the day after tomorrow. With luck, I'll be able to talk with Reyna Galeano." Justin nodded in approval.

"You seem to be on the right track," he commented. "I'll report to your mother this afternoon that you don't really need my services. I'm only sorry I won't be a part of this investigation."

At first, Gloria had gotten upset, suspecting that her mother had hired Justin not only to protect her, but also to solve the case for her. Then, Gloria realized that she herself should hire Justin to assist her; so, she asked him, "Why would this case interest you?"

"I don't often have an opportunity to do criminal investigation, and without question, this case intrigues me," he explained, then added, "You've already done most of the investigation but I would love to get a chance to follow it through to the end."

"I'd like to offer you that opportunity, but under certain conditions." Gloria paused. "No solo performances on your part. All decisions are mutually agreed upon. If there's anything to report, you inform me, not my mother—no matter how much she begs you. I'll be the one, of course, to pay your fees from now on."

"All right," Justin accepted the terms without hesitation. He was baffled by his own attitude since he had always preferred to work alone. In particular, he had managed so far to keep away from any amateur detectives. But this time, he actually found himself looking forward to working with Gloria.

After they agreed on the financial terms, they laid out a plan of action that would take Justin to Marysville the next morning while Gloria met with Otilia in Oakland.

The following day, as she drove to see Otilia, Gloria thought about Justin. Not only had she been favorably impressed by him, but he had also been highly recommended to Luisa who had hired him on behalf of Gloria's mother. An honest, astute investigator, he had a Master's in psychology, as well as five years of experience as a police officer in San Jose, and two years of investigative work with the Pacific Gold Insurance Company. "I don't see how we can go wrong," she said under her breath as she approached the Cisneros' residence.

A blue Mercedes was blocking the driveway, so Gloria parked on the street. Since she hadn't been at the house for a few months, she wondered if Lillian had a new car.

As usual, Elena, the housekeeper, greeted her at the door with a smile and inquired about Tania. On several occasions, over the years, Gloria's daughter had come with her to see Otilia, and the housekeeper had grown very fond of Tania. This time, Elena informed Gloria that Mrs. Juárez was on the phone, but asked her to wait in the solarium. This sunroom was really an enclosed extension of the sitting room, with large windows facing the bay. A sliding door connected it to the den, but that door was usually kept closed.

It was an unusually clear, cold day. The view of the bay was spectacular and Gloria delighted in the scene, letting her mind drift. The wind, a mere whisper that morning, had started blowing harder, driving away some of the clouds, chilling the air and filling it with the smell of eucalyptus and pine, the scent of Christmas. Tania had been born on a day like this. This would be their first Christmas without Darío, who had died two months after Tania's twentieth birthday.

Suddenly, Gloria's sorrow was interrupted by the sound of the aria "Un bel di" from *Madame Butterfly*. She turned towards the den. The Christmas tree stood next to the door between the den and the solarium and it offered Gloria a clear view of the scene in the room at the same time that it protected her from being seen by anyone in the den.

At first, Gloria only saw Lillian Cisneros. She was wearing a dark gold, silk jumpsuit and was sitting on a settee in front of a burning fireplace. Her face was pearled with perspiration.

Then Gloria detected someone else in the room. From her vantage point she could only glimpse the arm and hand of a man. Michael, she assumed. Then to Gloria's surprise, Paul Cisneros came into her line of vision. He was walking towards Lillian, carrying a glass with a small amount of a rather opaque liquid and offered it to her. She gulped down the contents like someone who has gone too long without water. Then she gave the glass back to Paul who put it down on the coffee table. Lillian tried to get up, but stumbled back on the settee, looking confused and frightened.

Gloria recalled that Otilia had referred to her "daughter's problem" in past conversations. If alcohol was indeed Lillian's problem, Gloria thought, Paul shouldn't be giving her a drink.

In a solicitous way, Paul made Lillian lie down, then covered her with an afghan and brushed her hair away from her face with his fingers. He then rewound the tape in the cassette deck near them and soon the heart-rending lyrics of "Un bel di" filled the air again. The music seemed to have a soothing effect on Lillian, for she immediately seemed to quiet down.

Paul stood there watching her for an instant, extending his right hand in front of him to straighten a ring he was wearing. Gloria drew back a little to avoid being seen as she watched him stop in front of the fireplace to glance up at the oil portrait of his mother and father above the mantle. Then, he threw his shoulders back. His arms and hands were jerking slightly. At the sound of a door closing upstairs, he took off his ring and picked up the glass. Putting both the ring and the glass in the pocket of his overcoat he slid into the coat, and swiftly walked out of the room.

What was in that glass that he had to take it with him, Gloria wondered, as she hurried towards the front of the house. By the time she reached the entryway, Paul was already pulling the front door quietly behind him. She was getting ready to check on Lillian when Otilia came down the stairs, looking quite troubled.

"Dr. Farber, Lilly's psychiatrist, wants to prescribe more tranquilizers for her. I can't believe the only treatment for my daughter's condition is a pill and nothing else," Otilia said. "I'm going to stop giving Lilly that medication," she continued in an even angrier tone. "I'll take full responsibility for my daughter from now on."

Otilia walked into the den and Gloria followed her. The room felt unusually warm. Yet, under the afghan, Lillian was now shaking and her face was moist, as if her body were fighting against giving in to a fever.

"I wish Michael were back," Otilia said, as she began to rub Lillian's legs while Gloria massaged her hands and arms.

"Where did Michael go?" Gloria asked.

"Where?" Lillian mumbled, without opening her eyes.

"He went to Solera," Otilia explained to her daughter, then turned to Gloria. "He was also planning to stop at an employment agency on his way back, to hire a nurse to be with Lilly at all times." Calling Gloria aside, she whispered, "I think Black Swan International Enterprises is in trouble. Michael might have to sell the winery and that has upset Lilly. At the moment, he and Paul are preparing for a board meeting scheduled for the day after tomorrow."

"Is that why Paul was just here?" Gloria asked.

"Paul was here?"

"I saw him here, in this room, with Lillian, giving her a drink," Gloria replied, before she realized there was no bar in the Cisneros' den.

"A drink? Lilly's not supposed to drink when she's under medication," Otilia exclaimed. Without giving Gloria a chance to explain further, she inquired. "How long ago was he here?"

"He had just walked out when you came down the stairs."

"I see," was all that Otilia said, but Gloria noticed the edge in her voice. Pulling the afghan over her daughter, who seemed now to be resting comfortably, Otilia began to move towards the door. She signaled for Gloria to follow her. Once outside, Otilia said in a low voice, "I don't want to leave Lilly alone. Would you mind if we have lunch here instead? I can ask Elena to prepare something quick for us and we can have a nice visit."

"I'd like that," Gloria assured her.

During lunch, Otilia hardly ate, talking instead about Lillian's state of mind and erratic behavior—including a delusion that little Michael needed her and that someone was following her, causing her to have two near-accidents in her car.

"I know something is very wrong with Lilly," Otilia said, winding up her tale. "I just ... don't know how to help her," she continued with a tremulous voice. "I don't fear anyone else is doing her harm. I'm rather afraid that Lilly is going over the edge on her own."

"Are you saying that she is disturbed enough to attempt taking her own life?" When Otilia nodded, Gloria asked, "What makes you think Lilly wants to kill herself?"

"I don't know the exact reason. It's difficult to tell, but I think there is something that's been driving her out of her mind slowly but surely over the years."

"That's interesting," Gloria noted. "A long time ago, Detective Kenyon seemed to share your concern about Lilly. He thought that she felt disproportionately responsible for her son's death."

Otilia folded her hands, then looked at Gloria directly. "It's true that my daughter's real problems began after little Michael was murdered because it was at that time that Lilly began to have severe bouts of depression and anxiety. I used to ask her to confide in me, and I tried to tell her that no matter what it was that was bothering her I would still love her. I would always stand by her, I reassured her. But Lilly never said anything and I finally stopped asking." Rubbing her chest with her hand, Otilia added, "Other people know what's behind her behavior. I'm almost sure Lilly has opened up to her friend Barbara."

"And to Michael?"

"No, I don't think so. He would have said something to me since he has been as much at a loss as I have regarding Lilly's emotional problems." Otilia paused and smoothed her hair, a gesture that always indicated to Gloria that Otilia was debating whether or not to tell her something. Otilia's right hand was trembling and she tried to steady it with her left one, but the shaking only got worse. Momentarily, she said, "But I suspect Lilly has opened up to Paul."

Gloria looked at Otilia's forehead, where every wrinkle seemed to have deepened in a matter of minutes. "What makes you say that?" she asked, rubbing her friends' hands lightly.

The older woman still hesitated to say what was on her mind. Sensing Otilia's need to share whatever it was that troubled her, Gloria encouraged her, "Once, when Luisa and I went to see you at Solera, Paul was there also. I remember two things about our brief visit with him. That he was really a lonely, vulnerable man and that you didn't care very much for him. Then, just awhile ago, you seemed quite upset by the fact that he had been with Lilly in the den."

"You're right to a certain extent," Otilia conceded, "but it isn't that I don't like him. I just don't like the way he treats Lilly. He seems to protect her but in a very ... unusual way. And she seems to listen to him. I mean—I guess she humors him, but not in the same way that she tries to please Michael. Sometimes I feel that maybe she and Paul ... Oh, God forbid!"

Unprepared for what Otilia was suggesting, Gloria was quiet for a moment, then tried to reassure her that Lillian wasn't in love with her own brother-in-law. "About Paul ... " Gloria began to say, then changed her mind.

"Go on," Otilia prompted her. "What about Paul?"

Gloria told her friend about the meeting between Lillian and Paul earlier that afternoon. "Then," she commented, "I was very surprised when he rushed out of here as soon as he heard someone coming."

"Not as surprised as I was to hear he'd been here." Otilia looked away but her voice betrayed her contempt as she remarked, "This man thinks that he can do as he pleases. He's involved Lilly in ... in some kind of affair." She turned to Gloria, and said, "I'm going to need your help."

Delighted that Otilia had decided to take up some action, Gloria immediately inquired, "How can I help?"

"I'm not exactly sure at this point. All I know is that I must protect Lilly."

"If Detective Kenyon and you are right, and Lilly's problems started at the time little Michael was murdered," Gloria reasoned, "then, perhaps we should concentrate on finding out who killed your grandson and what were the motives for this cowardly act?" She knew she had to find a way to tell Otilia about the information she had collected over the years.

"You really think there's a connection between what happened to my grandson and what's now happening to my daughter, don't you?" Otilia was intrigued.

"Yes, I do."

Gloria paused. Afraid that there might not be a better opportunity, she immediately decided to tell Otilia everything she knew about her grandson's murder. She summarized for her older friend the data contained in Kenyon's files and the possible participation of a Brazilian brotherhood in Mando's and little Michael's murders.

Then, she related her meeting with Father Stewart and concluded by stating there was a strong possibility that Michael was really Cecilia Castro-Biddle's son. That she might have been the person who abducted little Michael from Otilia's house.

Gloria paused, waiting for her friend's reaction. When Otilia didn't respond, Gloria went on, "But I still can't figure out who put Cecilia up to her wrong-doing."

"I've known Michael was adopted," Otilia said after awhile. "Nonetheless, I hadn't any idea—and I don't think anyone else does—that Michael's mother was this Mrs. Castro-Biddle, or why she would resort to such horrible actions." Waving her hand, she continued, "Mind you, in this family, no one has ever talked openly about either Michael's adoption or about his abduction. Their attitude has always surprised me. C'mon, we live in the twentieth century. Why try to keep the adoption a secret?"

"You must have an idea why they've been so hush-hush about it."

"I'm not sure," Otilia shook her head. "Unless it has to do with old man Bjorgun's attitude towards Michael. Paul hasn't said it in so many words, but I think that's what he's meant whenever he's told me that his grandfather preferred him—Paul—because they both came from the same line."

"Any chance he's also adopted?"

"Not Paul. He was born in Berkeley. He showed me his birth certificate years ago when I had first met the family. I thought it was a strange thing for a young man to do at the time." After a brief pause, Otilia expressed her frustration, "I have this awful feeling that I must do something quickly to protect my daughter, but I don't know where to begin ... Perhaps with a visit to Paul's house or a talk with him. I don't know."

"I'm not exactly sure that a visit to his house is the best way to find out what's happening between him and Lillian," Gloria commented. "Besides, how would we get in his house? Wouldn't the servants or Paul be at home?"

"Paul doesn't get home until after nine o'clock," Otilia said, suddenly sitting straight up in her chair. "Lee, the house manager, and Bruna, the maid, will be home. But Lee probably won't think it strange that we drop in. I've been there other times to pick up things, mostly with Lilly or Michael. But if we go through with it, we would have to be there before eight this evening. Lee leaves the house to walk the dog at about that time. The maid is usually gone by then too."

"You're serious about this, aren't you?" Gloria clarified, but warned, "Unless we know what we're looking for, it will be useless to pay a visit to Paul's house." She proposed instead, "Why don't I call you later? We can talk again about a plan of action then."

Otilia agreed.

Later that afternoon, Gloria called Otilia as she had promised. Michael was still at the office, Otilia told her. Apparently, things at Black Swan International had reached a critical stage and Michael and Paul had to prepare for the company's board meeting. The nurse Michael had hired had just arrived and Otilia wanted to be there when the nurse talked to Lilly's doctor. Given the complications, Otilia suggested they postpone their trip to Paul's house until the following morning.

Throughout the afternoon, Gloria had been unable to get Lillian out of her mind. If Darío were alive, she thought, he would immediately be able to tell what was causing Lillian's symptoms.

Not wanting to give in to the sadness pressing around her eyelids at the memory of her husband, Gloria decided to go into Darío's library. She pulled out a medical encyclopedia and sat down by the window to read and await news from Justin. Then, for a short while, she slept.

NINETEEN

Retrospect of Darkness

At about an hour before noon, Justin arrived at Sylvia Castañeda's address. As he approached the porch he noticed a sign above the steps: Rand Miller and Associates, Tax Consultants. Next to the mailbox, delivery service carriers were advised not to disturb the occupants of the house and to drop mail or parcels at the office in the rear.

Justin knocked at the door of a back cottage that said "Office." A young man peeked through the window next to the door, then buzzed him in.

"I'm sorry," the young man said, from behind a reception window. "We open at one p.m. on Fridays," he continued. "Did you have an appointment with Rand or one of the associates? If so, I wasn't told. And he won't be back until this afternoon."

"No, I didn't." Justin paused. The young man didn't seem to be in any hurry to get back to work, so Justin decided to try to get some information about Sylvia out of him. "Actually, you might be able to help me ... What's your name?"

"William Harrison—Bill."

"Nice to meet you, Bill. I'm Justin Escobar. I don't really know Mr. Miller," he explained. "I'm actually looking for Reyna Miller's mother—Sylvia. Do you know her?"

"Mrs. Castañeda?" Bill asked, and immediately added, "Sure I know her. She's down at Little Red Shoes, her children's clothing store on Main Street. I can give you directions on how to get there if you'd like ... "

"Is Mrs. Miller home? I have some packages for the family from Mrs. Hinkle, their friend and former neighbor in Santa Monica."

"She sure is," Bill volunteered. "C'mon, Mr. Escobar. I'll take you to her." Stepping out of the reception booth, he opened the front door.

Smiling at Bill's eagerness to stray from the office, Justin said jokingly, "I hope I'm not taking you away from your duties."

The young man shook his head, and they headed towards the main house.

Justin rather liked the idea of letting Bill take care of the introductions. They knocked on the front door of the main house.

When Reyna opened the door, Bill introduced Justin and explained why he had come to see Sylvia. Reyna looked at Justin with some hesitation, then invited them both to come in the house. Justin excused himself and went to his van to bring Mrs. Hinkle's gifts while Bill walked into the kitchen to get a drink of water.

After Justin delivered the presents, Reyna invited him into the living room for coffee. He sat in an easy chair away from the entrance while she took a place on the sofa closer to the front door.

Sensing her apprehension, Justin took out his P.I. identification and the piece of paper where he'd written Gloria's and Luisa's phone numbers, and put both items on the coffee table.

"So, Mr. Escobar. How is it that you know Betsy? Are you one of her neighbors?" Reyna asked without preambles, but observed his movements closely.

Aware that a visit from anyone even remotely connected with her life in Los Angeles was a matter of concern to Reyna, he decided that being straightforward with her was the best approach. So he said, "You might remember Gloria Damasco and Luisa Cortez." He paused when he heard Reyna's gasp, then continued, "Gloria might be in danger. And I've come here on her behalf to seek your help."

Reyna's face turned pale, then color returned to her cheeks. Still, she said nothing.

"We need to find out," he went on, "about your first husband's connections to an organization in Brazil, a group known perhaps as the Brazilian brotherhood." He said this perfunctorily, but watched for her reaction. "We'd be grateful if you could tell us anything at all you remember that might help us identify who they are."

Stunned at being faced with a situation she had feared for years, Reyna couldn't begin to articulate even a simple protest. Her cheeks paled even more when she heard the kitchen door open and close. Justin realized that Bill was going back to the office. An instant later, a cat strolled into the living room and jumped on the sofa, but Reyna caught him and swiftly put him back on the floor. Justin noticed her hands were shaking.

Allergic to cats, Justin prayed he would not start sneezing, so she would not be frightened any more than she already was. But almost immediately he felt the ticklish wave of a first sneeze, and his hand moved up to block it.

As he expected, Reyna got up, then began to retreat towards the coat closet by the front door. All the time she was moving, she kept her eye on him. At the closet door, with a trembling hand, she turned the knob and opened the door, but did not move further.

Knowing that she might have a weapon hidden there, Justin didn't attempt to get up. Keeping a steady, low tone, he said, "I know all these years you've been trying to forget what you went through in L.A. and I can also tell that you've lived in constant fear that one day a stranger like me would come to your door. That he would be looking for the Reyna that was married to Joel Galeano—the man who was an accomplice in the Cisneros boy's murder." He paused to gain a hint from Reyna, but she was simply standing silently by the open closet door. Her hands were still in plain view, but her eyes were moving rapidly, debating whether to go for the weapon or the front door.

"I wish you no harm, Mrs. Miller," Justin tried to reassure her. "If I did, you must admit, I would not have come to your house to talk. Then, he added, as he slid the piece of paper down the table towards her, "On that slip, you'll find Gloria's number. I can leave now and come back in ten minutes if you'd rather call her first."

"What you're talking about happened such a long time ago," Reyna finally said, in a raspy voice. "I thought the *murderer* had committed suicide."

"Joel was responsible for Mando Cadena's death but he didn't murder little Michael. Someone else killed the boy."

Relieved to find out that Joel had not killed the child, she let out a long sigh. Then, closing the door, she walked back to her place on the sofa. "I knew that sooner or later my children and I would have to pay for Joel's bad deeds," she explained.

"Believe me, Mrs. Miller," Justin said reassuringly. "You and your children have nothing to fear from me. I'm not here to harm you. I'm here to ask for your help."

"How can I help?"

"Please, tell me as much as you remember about those few weeks before the murders." Justin's nose itched and he rubbed it.

Not knowing where to begin, she hesitated. He tried to assist her by asking, "When did you first notice Joel was involved in suspicious activities?"

"It was about three months before the Moratorium march," she began, "when he started depositing very large amounts in our account. He had never gotten that much money for his freelance work. When I inquired about it, he told me he had been able to sell several of his articles and photo-essays on L.A. gangs to some national magazines. He also said that a major press had offered him a hefty advance for a book of his articles and photos."

"What happened then to make you suspect something wasn't quite right?"

"As it got closer to the march, Joel began to get many strange calls."

"Strange in what way?"

"A couple of times, someone called from Rio de Janeiro. The day before the Moratorium march, there was a call in the middle of the night. I took the call and I talked to an operator with a heavy German accent. I assumed the call was coming from Germany."

"Do you by any chance remember anything about those conversations?"

"They were always about money," Reyna answered promptly. "Two days after the Moratorium—the night that the young Santos got killed—another call from Germany came in. This time, I pretended to go back to bed, but stayed just outside the door and listened in on Joel's conversation. He talked about not using a gun but a knife—something like that. That he had done things according to plan, and promised he would be sending the photos he had taken as proof. That's when I really became suspicious.

"After he went back to sleep, I got his keys and went into the darkroom. I searched through everything he had there. Then I couldn't believe what I found." Reyna's eyes became moist. "There were photos of the dead child and of the young Santos, dead also, with a knife lying next to him. I was shocked when I recognized Joel's knife, the one he had gotten in Viet Nam during his tour of duty there. I had dusted all his war memorabilia often enough to recognize the markings on its handle. How can Joel be so foolish as to leave his own knife next to a body, I thought at first; then I remembered the caller had asked for proof of what Joel had done. I kept staring at the photos for a long time, unable to accept what I had before my very eyes."

Reyna looked at Justin, then lowered her eyes. "I guess I felt responsible for some of Joel's actions. I felt quite guilty after I found out what he had done to get money for us ... " Reyna began to cry. Justin gave her time to regain her composure.

"About five o'clock in the morning," she continued, "I made up my mind to burn the photos and the negatives. Exhausted and confused as I was, I then began to feel frightened—really paranoid—and sure that I could never again trust Joel, that I would forever be a slave to my fear of him. I guess that's when I decided to keep some of the negatives to protect myself and the children if he or anyone else ever came after us.

"The children and the few belongings I was taking were already in the car when I remembered I did not have the checkbook in my purse, so I went back for it. I was almost out the door when he walked into the living room. I was petrified. At first, he was shocked to see his photos burning in the fireplace. Then he started coming at me. I grabbed the scissors and stabbed him in the face, then ran out and drove away as fast as I could." Reyna wiped her tears with the back of her hand.

"Do you still have those negatives?" Justin asked after awhile.

Unable to speak, Reyna could only nod.

"Would you mind letting me have them?" Justin ventured.

When she hesitated, he promised, "I will try my best to keep you and your children out of any further investigation. This might be a way to close the book on your life with Galeano."

He waited.

Without saying a word, Reyna went to her bedroom and came back a short time later with a manila envelope. She handed it to Justin. "They're all in there," she said.

Then she went to the front door and opened it. "My husband will be back soon. I'd rather he doesn't find you here when he comes home."

"You're a very courageous woman, Mrs. Miller," Justin said, with a smile. "I'm sure Gloria and Luisa will be as grateful as I am for what you've just done. Thanks." He shook her hand and reached for the doorknob.

"No," Reyna responded, "I'm the one who's grateful. Thank *you*." She smiled for the first time since Justin had walked into her house. Then, she even waved as he started up the street towards downtown.

After drinking a potful of coffee and shopping for some allergy medicine, Justin started back to the Bay Area. He tapped the manila envelope and smiled. Gloria would be pleased, he was sure.

At six o'clock, he showed up at Gloria's door. Although he was still occasionally sneezing, and his eyes were red, he smiled as he waited for her to open the door.

"I gather you found Reyna Galeano," Gloria stated as she studied his face, debating whether or not she should check his forehead for a fever. She decided against doing that.

"Yes," Justin said. Clearing his throat, he proceeded to give her a brief account of his exchange with Reyna. Then, he pulled out the envelope with the negatives.

"Now we're in business!" she exclaimed.

Justin smiled. "I have a darkroom at home and I'll print the photos later tonight," he reassured her. Then he inquired, "How did your meeting with Otilia go?"

"Fine," she replied, then she told him what had happened at the Cisneros' household; then, she described Lillian's condition. She concluded by telling him about the visit to Paul's house that she and Otilia were planning for the next day.

"I thought it might be a good idea to check out the servants' routine anyway," she explained. "So, I figured you and I could take a look around Pacific Heights this evening—a little reconnoitering, that's all."

"Good," Justin agreed. "It never hurts to plan ahead." He rubbed his nose with a rapid motion.

Gloria looked closely at his eyes. "You're in no condition to drive. I better do it. Let's go in your van though," she said and signaled him to follow her outside. He waved his finger indicating he had no objections and got in the passenger side.

They rode off in silence, across the Bay Bridge, looking at the city in its Christmas splendor. The Golden Gate Bridge rose magnificently in the distance as they drove on to the next scheduled encounter with fate.

TWENTY
Windswept Heights/Cloudless Views

The two-story Southern style house stood softly-lit and unmenacing under cloudless skies. Gloria and Justin parked about fifty feet from the house, on the opposite side of the street. Twenty minutes after they arrived, a man stepped out with a German shepherd on a leash, and dog and man got into the station wagon in the driveway.

Justin and Gloria slid down on the seat to avoid being seen, and the car took off without the driver paying any attention to them. A few minutes later a middle-aged woman came out of the house and walked to her car parked a few feet from them. "The maid," Justin murmured close to Gloria's ear, sending a tingling sensation down her neck.

Although Gloria hadn't thought of doing anything more than observing the comings and goings around the house from a distance, as soon as she thought it was safe, she got out of the car and began walking towards the house. "Gloria," she heard Justin whisper, behind her. "Gloria," he said again—louder this time—as he got hold of her jacket sleeve and pulled her around. "*¿Estás loca?*"

"No, I'm not crazy," she snapped. "You don't have to come if you don't want to."

"All right," he snorted. "Let me get my gear." He drew a circle in the air, indicating he'd meet her in back of the house. If Paul's house manager took the dog as usual to the Marina district as Otilia had said he would, then he'd take about forty minutes to come back. But they had no way of knowing this for sure.

"We should count on no more than twenty minutes," Justin told Gloria while he set the alarm on his wrist watch to go off in fifteen minutes.

He moved quietly around the side of the house while Gloria tried the back door. It was locked, she soon found out, so she went to see what Justin was doing. He pointed at the metal-covered cable running parallel to the electrical wires into the meter box. "Burglary alarm."

151

They circled again to the back of the house.

"That's illegal," Gloria said when she saw him begin to manipulate the single bolt lock of the kitchen door with a device that had flat and hook-like ends and was taped to a slim pen flashlight.

He chuckled as if to say, "Look who's worrying about the law now."

"It's taking too long," Gloria complained, leaning over his shoulder.

"This ain't TV, you know? Patience."

"Aren't you worried about the alarm?"

"I don't think it's on. Look around. Two windows are open," he said under his breath "in two different sections of the house."

"Where?"

"Take a look. Upstairs. Quiet, please."

A few seconds later, Justin gently pushed the door open. He reached under his jacket, took out a regular flashlight and lit the way.

He disappeared into a bathroom while Gloria checked the master bedroom. Although the room was only comfortably warm, she began to perspire profusely. Trying to cool down, she sat on the bed, fanning herself. Suddenly, she thought she heard voices, then a whimper.

She closed her eyes and a young boy's voice began to say, "She loves *you*."

"That's not true," the voice of an older boy answered.

As she sat there, Gloria sensed that the voices she was hearing were those of Paul and Michael as children—perhaps at ages six and ten.

"You hate me too," Paul claimed.

"I don't."

"You made me eat that rabbit shit."

"I didn't make you eat anything. You told me Grandfather said you were braver than me. You said that you could eat it and I couldn't." (Laughter) "Was it good?" (More laughter).

"Mommy hates me. You do too. She punished me but she didn't punish *you*, Michael." (Whimpering. Silence.)

"Did you kill him, Paul? You loved that rabbit so much. How could you kill him?"

"I didn't do it. You killed him."

Paul's whimpering turned to loud crying, then became a continuous groan, like that of a small dying animal.

Although her vision lasted only a few seconds, Gloria had immediately felt young Paul's pain and loneliness.

Remembering that she and Justin had to be out of there before Paul's house manager returned, Gloria wiped her tears and quickly inspected the dressing room and another small closet. There wasn't anything that even resembled the box Otilia had described to her at Solera on the day she and Luisa had first met Paul.

Uncertain about what it was Otilia hoped to find at Paul's house, Gloria searched first through the chest of drawers and a small secretary. Then, on the wall above the bed, she noticed the oil portrait of a man who, she assumed, was Soren Bjorgun. Next to the portrait of the older man was a large photograph of Paul at his present age. The two men resembled each other so much it was uncanny. They shared not only the same physical attributes, but even the look in their eyes.

Above the desk, next to a framed chart with illustrations of the most popular handguns and revolvers, Gloria saw a large map of Brazil, also framed. A small "x" marked a spot somewhere in the Matto Grosso area. She stared at it in disbelief. But, as she looked down, the Smith and Wesson .357 on the night table dispelled any illusions of misjudgement on her part. Feeling a bit lightheaded, she leaned on the table and closed her eyes. She felt the icy grip of fingers against her neck, and she opened her eyes immediately.

Coming out of the room, she almost bumped into Justin as he was stepping out of another bedroom. Hearing the sound of his watch alarm as she went down the service stairs, she thought that Justin was right behind her. Instead, he had cautiously gone down the main stairs to the ground floor. Checking out the study, he noticed the strong box next to the desk. Suspecting there was also a wall safe, he regretted not being able to find out what both safes contained. Then, as he was rushing out of the room, he glimpsed a smaller metal box on the computer table. Tempted to take it, he had to struggle with himself to leave it where it was.

Outside the house, Gloria crouched under the kitchen window. Her entire body was dulled by the gusty arctic wind that blew into this area of San Francisco as it opened to the sea. Rewrapping her scarf around her neck and ears, she looked up at the clear sky, then at the three stars on Orion's belt. Her grandmother used to tell her those stars were the Magi, bringing presents to all the children on earth. On a starry night like this, Gloria thought, how can one believe death might be only the length of an arm away.

A few seconds later, a dog barked in the distance just as Justin was stepping out of the kitchen door. "C'mon," she prompted. "He's coming back."

"That's not the bark of a German shepherd," he said calmly. "Besides, we wouldn't be able to hear it with the car windows rolled up. But it's time to go anyway," he said and pressed her elbow. "I'll drive this time."

They were barely inside the van when another car pulled up in front of the house. "Not the bark of a German shepherd, right?" Gloria teased him. He laughed. They kept out of sight, then drove away as soon as it was safe.

On the way home, Gloria told Justin about the visions she had seen, and about the map of Brazil and the gun chart, then mentioned seeing the gun on the night table. "By the way, do you carry a gun?" she asked him.

"Not on me, but I do own one," he said. "Lest I forget, tomorrow, when you come back with Otilia, look in the study for a small metal box. It might be the box that contained Michael Sr.'s personal papers, the one Otilia saw Paul rummaging through once?"

Reaching under his seat, Justin pulled out a paper bag. "I have a present for you. I found this in the medicine chest." He dangled the paper bag in front of her.

Taking off her gloves, Gloria opened the bag, then reached into it. Contact with cold glass made her shiver. But the wave moving up her chest and arms to her neck was warm, as she pulled out a small bottle. Then she turned on the flashlight and read the words *"Elixir de Pereira/Elixir de Juventude"* printed on the label.

Impulsively, she reached out for Justin's arm and squeezed it to express her gratitude and happiness. Every muscle in his upper arm tensed up as a tingling sensation spread up his shoulder and neck. He relaxed almost immediately after but she had already removed her hand. She again flashed the light on the label, which resembled the label on the bottle of health tonic Gloria's grandmother used to drink. It pictured a dandy looking man with straight, slicked-back hair, striking an elegant pose in coat-tails and two-tone shoes, his hat in one hand and a walking stick in the other—undoubtedly the portrait of high fashion in Latin American countries at the turn of the century. The label was printed on paper that appeared to date from that time as well. The liquid in the bottle was so thick it was almost opaque.

For an instant, the memory of Lillian gulping down a glass of a liquid resembling the elixir in color and texture flashed through Gloria's mind.

She opened the bottle. The mellow fragrance of vanilla fooled her into believing the elixir was also sweet-tasting. A drop of it proved otherwise. It had a metallic, slightly piquant but not disagreeable taste.

"If you don't have a fever, what would happen to you if you ingest a febrifuge—you know—a substance used to bring down fever?" Gloria asked Justin.

"It's safe to assume that your temperature would go down to a critical low," he answered.

"Hypothermia," Gloria exclaimed, remembering what she had read in Darío's medical encyclopedia earlier in the afternoon. As she put the bottle of elixir back in the bag, she whispered, "Thanks."

Justin acknowledged her gratitude with a shrug of his shoulder and a smile.

Thirty minutes later, the enormous loading cranes at the Port of Oakland came into view. Gloria imagined Michael Cisneros laboring beyond them, in Jingle Town, to save Black Swan from a takeover by Anaconda Sur International. She also wondered about Lillian. The thought that Lillian's blood might literally be freezing in her veins sent chills up Gloria's spine.

TWENTY-ONE

Dark Swan/Light Swan

After returning from Paul's house, Gloria and Justin went to Justin's place. Before his parents died, it had been a one-family residence, but he had converted it into two separate spaces. An inside door connected the upstairs office and its adjoining darkroom to the downstairs flat which served as Justin's living quarters.

Almost immediately, they began to print the photos from the negatives Reyna had given him. They set up enlargements from various sections of the photos to dry in the upstairs darkroom while downstairs they began to study the first set of photos.

Justin had laid them on the carpet, next to the fireplace, and while he prepared dinner, Gloria began to look at the photos. Of special interest to her were Joel's shots of the National Chicano Moratorium riot. She picked up one of the photos of Mando staring out from the crowd. The killer's back appeared in several of the photos but she noticed that none of them showed his face.

Waiting for the next batch of photos to dry, Gloria looked around Justin's apartment. It was cozy and looked clean and organized. Neatly arranged next to the living room window were a few weights and a rowing machine. With the exception of *"Los perros de medianoche,"* an oil painting by Malaquías Montoya on the wall opposite the fireplace, the artwork in Justin's apartment consisted of photographs he had taken of buildings, fountains, playgrounds and other outdoor places. Some had children or older people in them, but many others lacked even a shadow of a human presence.

As she was looking at Justin's work, Gloria heard the bell of the timer in the darkroom. "Do you mind if I take a look at the rest of the pictures now?"

"Be my guest," he answered from the kitchen. "Why don't you bring them downstairs? Bring the magnifying glass as well."

Once Gloria had brought the new materials downstairs, she began to group the photos by events.

"Justin, come and see them," she called out with excitement.

"In a minute," he replied. A short time later, he joined her in the living room.

She called his attention to an enlargement showing a banner with the letters *Irmandade brazileira para a justiça mundial,* no doubt the real name of the Brazilian brotherhood. The emblem with the lion's paw was visible at the top. A number of the pictures were of a training camp in a tropical forest. Looking closely at some of the men in another photo, Gloria noticed they were wearing fatigues. Rifles hung from their shoulders. Since their faces were covered by olive green and black paint, Gloria had a hard time trying to imagine what they would look like stripped of their camouflage. Justin had made an enlargement of the face and hands of one of the men. Although it was a bit blurry, one could still make out a ring with a lion's head on the man's finger.

Justin picked up the enlargement showing the man's painted face. He handed it to Gloria, who raised an eyebrow but remained silent. Without saying a word, he went back into the kitchen to check on their dinner.

"In view of this new development," he called out, "what do you suggest we do now?"

"I wish we could let Michael Cisneros take a look at all the documents and photos," Gloria said as she took a deep breath, trying to steady the beating of her heart. "More realistically, we ourselves might have to set a trap for this cunning member of the *Irmandade,*" she murmured, tapping at the face of the man on the enlargement.

To her surprise, Justin shouted from the kitchen, "For that, we will need Otilia's help."

"Then, I better take all the evidence to Otilia. I'm sure she'll go along with us after she sees these photos." Trying to warm her hands, she breathed on them with her open mouth, then extended them towards the burning logs in the fireplace. "Why don't we talk to Otilia together?" she suggested.

Justin agreed as he announced that their meal was ready. Dinner was a delicious chicken soup, a green salad and quesadillas made of *queso fresco* covered with a creamy *chile colorado* sauce. Half a mug of Bohemia for each of them complemented the meal perfectly.

Although Gloria expected the usual "from my mother" response, she asked Justin, "Where did you learn to cook like this?"

"From my uncle, Tito Garro." Justin cleared the table and headed towards the kitchen.

Gloria recognized the name immediately. Before his death in a car accident, Tito Garro had been one of the most famous California chefs, a delightful attraction at his restaurant in Monterey. "That explains your good taste," she teased him. He was pleased.

Sometime later, the grandfather clock in Justin's office upstairs chimed the first hour of the day. Since she had been going nearly eighteen hours non-stop, Gloria could have expected to feel tired. Instead, as she got ready to head on home she suddenly felt full of energy.

Justin walked her to her car and waited until she drove off. When she started down the familiar route, she had every intention of going home to a warm shower and bed. But just a few blocks away from Justin's home, she decided to head towards the corner of Monterey and Leimert, asking herself for the hundredth time why she couldn't stay away from the spot.

As she approached the corner, she automatically threw a quick look at the vacant lot where Michael and Lillian's home had once stood. The extremely bright lights of an oncoming car blinded her, but she still managed to catch a glimpse of a blue Mercedes Benz as it headed out of the old Cisneros' driveway, making a left turn on Leimert.

Unable to see well, she pulled up to the curb and closed her eyes to wait out the momentary blindness. In a flash, she glimpsed Lillian Cisneros' face. A hand wearing a ring with a lion's head—the same hand she had just seen on one of the photo enlargements—wrapped around Lillian's neck. When she opened her eyes again, the blue Mercedes was gone.

By now, she knew Leimert and most of the streets around that area very well; so, rushing to the one spot where she knew the car could reappear, she was pleased with herself when she recognized the blue Mercedes. It was heading down Park Boulevard towards the MacArthur Freeway, which connected to the Oakland-San Francisco-Bay Bridge.

Realizing that *he* was going home, she decided not to follow. Instead, she headed for her own house. Was it to see Paul Cisneros exit from that lot that she had been drawn to that spot so often? What had he been doing there at that late hour? She and Justin would have to look for the answer in that lot the following morning, Gloria thought, as she drove up her driveway.

As soon as she saw her daughter Tania's car parked in front of the house, she remembered she had promised to call Tania and Luisa as soon as she returned from San Francisco. In dealing with all the new developments, she had forgotten to do that. They had surely gotten worried, she figured, as she walked in and saw her daughter and her friend fast asleep on the living room carpet under a comforter. The embers in the fireplace creaked softly when the cold draft reached them.

"Good watchwomen you are," she whispered in her daughter's ear. "C'mon, honey, let's get you to bed."

"Will you be here in the morning?" Tania mumbled.

"Of course, I'll be here in the morning," Gloria reassured her.

"Night, Mom."

Luisa rolled over. She began to rub her wrist and to adjust a bandage wrapped around it.

"What did the doctor say about your wrist?" Gloria inquired.

"I can't work. I'm not s'pposed to lift anything or put any stress on my wrist. He says it's better if I don't drive for awhile. That's why I asked Tania to bring me," she explained.

After putting two more logs in the fireplace, Gloria turned to Luisa, "Want me to take you home?"

"Would you mind if I stay? Tania can give me a ride home in the morning. I'm very tired and I'd rather not be out now or make you go out in the cold." Luisa looked at Gloria rubbing her eyes. "You look exhausted too. I bet you've been going all day without much rest."

"Uh-huh." Intending to enjoy the warm and peaceful glow of the fire for a little while, Gloria lay down on the spot that Tania had occupied.

In a minute, Luisa was fast asleep again. Her rhythmic breathing formed a triad with the ticking of the clock in the dining room and the sound of the northern gale still thrashing hill and shore.

With her eyes closed Gloria listened to that music until there was nothing but a softly pulsating darkness in her head.

Suddenly, out of the quietude, Luisa's voice rose. Gloria looked for her but all she could see were the acacias in bloom, like yellow flames along the road. Then, Luisa was there, beyond a patch of wild berries, the bandage on her wrist and her blouse full of purple blackberry stains.

Gloria tried to walk through the patch of vines, but their thorns drove painfully into her thighs and legs, so she went back to look for a way around the prickly lot. When she was finally at the spot where she had seen Luisa, her friend was gone, and in her place stood Otilia, looking twenty years younger and holding little Michael David by the hand.

The following morning, Gloria woke up to the smell of a steaming cup of coffee that Luisa was offering her. Tania had breakfast ready for them. As they enjoyed the food and each other's company for a short while, Gloria tried to avoid talking about the things that she and Justin had discovered the night before. Then, Tania and Luisa were gone.

As she waited for Justin to pick her up, Gloria noticed the wind had died down to a gentle breeze. Clouds began to show their dark undulating bellies. Soft winter rain would begin falling by morning's end bringing chaos on roads and bridges *and* hope to everyone in a Bay Area that had already been experiencing a drought for two years.

TWENTY-TWO

Prelude to a Showdown

An hour before Gloria's scheduled meeting with Otilia, she and Justin drove up to the empty lot on Leimert and Monterey. After a thorough search, they found a spot that looked as if it'd been dug up recently, then carefully covered up again. But the earth in the hole was still loose enough to roughly calculate its dimensions.

"Whatever was buried here was narrow and long. A cylinder, perhaps," Justin commented. "I wonder what it is Paul has in such a container that he couldn't keep in his safes at home." He scratched his head. "More important, why is he digging this cylinder out now? And at night too?" Justin looked inquisitively at Gloria, who shook her head, then began to walk back to the car.

"While we find an answer to that question, I suggest we stay close to Lillian," she told Justin when he caught up with her.

They quickly made their way up to the Cisneros' house. Gloria knew something was afoot when Elena, the housekeeper, informed them that "Mrs. Cisneros and Mrs. Juárez" had left for Solera, in the Napa Valley, earlier that morning. As she said that, the housekeeper had a peculiar look in her eyes and tilted her head a few times. Realizing that Elena was trying to tell her something, she wondered if perhaps the housekeeper had been asked to lie about Otilia and Lillian's trip.

"Mr. Cisneros would also like to talk to you two, at his office," Elena told them. "He's free at eleven."

Gloria concluded that Otilia had perhaps tried to talk to Michael about their findings, and that he had gotten upset with the news that concerned him directly.

Then, as they drove away from the Cisneros' house, Gloria thought she saw a slit open in the window drapes. Although she suspected that mother and daughter were still in the house, she figured Otilia was probably pretending to follow someone's directions in order to protect Lillian.

161

Concerned primarily with the confrontation they were about to have with Michael Cisneros, Justin offered no comments when she told him about her suspicion.

The two of them showed up at Black Swan International just before eleven, but they had to wait for Michael for quite a while before they were shown into his office.

On the few occasions Gloria had been to his company, Michael had been a most affable host. But this time, she came face to face with a stern and angry man.

Trying not to show her apprehension, Gloria glanced at Justin, who was standing very still, staring back at Michael. Then, she cleared her throat and blurted out, "Your brother Paul killed your son." Gloria was surprised at her own words. All the time, she had been afraid to voice the name of the killer—to announce his guilt—almost as if in doing so, she would unleash an awesome power, a savage god that would demand her life in payment for her transgression. Yet, suddenly the words were pouring out of her mouth. "You must have been aware that he hated you." Michael stared coldly at her. She went on, "Weren't you aware of your brother's actions? Didn't you ever suspect he might wish harm to you and Lillian?"

"You have no right to upset my wife and my mother-in-law, and to come here throwing accusations around!" Michael glared at both of them.

"Why did you call us here, Mr. Cisneros?" Justin asked, trying to remain calm. "Don't you want to hear what we have to say?"

"All of that is beside the point now," Michael told Justin, then turned to Gloria. "You have forced me to ask you to leave right this minute! And, please, stay away from my wife."

"They're not unfounded accusations, Mr. Cisneros," Justin said in a deliberately polite tone as he took out the large envelope that contained copies of the photos, the newspaper clippings and the coroner's report. He emptied the contents on Michael's desk. "I'm sure you can fill in the gaps to whatever is missing here."

"This is the coroner's analysis of ... " Gloria began to explain, then stopped abruptly. Michael was staring at her with sullen anger, but there was also pain—perhaps even fear—in his eyes.

"Of your son's blood." Justin finished the sentence for her. Taking out the bottle of tonic, he showed it to Michael, who drew his head back as if to avoid an object aimed at him. "It contained traces of the substance in this elixir, which comes from Brazil." Justin continued. "Your brother goes often to Brazil. He's the only one who drinks this stuff."

For a few seconds Michael seemed to assess the validity of what he was being told. While verbally he didn't deny anything he had heard, he nonetheless pressed one of the buttons in the intercom. Justin and Gloria looked at one another, then got ready to leave before security threw them out.

"Many years ago," Gloria started to tell Michael in a quiet voice, "Paul took your son's life in exchange for the love he felt your mother denied him. I'm making an educated guess, but I think he also felt you robbed him of your father's respect when you were asked to head the company." Her heart began to step up its pace and her breathing faltered.

"Please stop! Do you really expect me to believe that my brother killed my son because he hates me?" Michael shook his head. "My brother loves me," he stated categorically.

While he spoke, Gloria took deep breaths, then began to speak fast— afraid that her voice would thin out. "In some weird, distorted way, he loves you. You're right. But he also hates you and he hates himself for loving you. He won't kill you. He'll kill everyone *you* love. He'll destroy everything you've built. Look at how he has gained control of your company." Her last remark was sheer speculation, but it seemed to have struck a chord with Michael.

Fear again moved swiftly across his gaze. "But that's insane. Why in Heaven's name would he do that for?"

The security guard knocked at the door and Justin threw it open. "No need to bother. We're leaving," he told the guard, as he pushed Gloria out gently by the elbow. Turning to look at Michael, he suggested, "Please think about what we've told you."

Knowing that she was putting both Justin and herself at risk, Gloria's last words to Michael were, "Keep the photos and reports. I beg you to look at everything before you make up your own mind."

The security guard escorted them to the entrance. When they were leaving the Black Swan International's parking lot, Paul Cisneros drove up in his blue Mercedes and stopped in front of the office building. He got out and began to walk up the flight of stairs. The attendant went to park the car.

"You think Michael will tell him about us?" Gloria asked, but she wasn't seeking an answer so much from Justin as from herself.

"That's what you had in mind, didn't you? Not a very good plan, Gloria." Justin shook his head. "It's obvious you want him to find you."

Gloria had to trust that Michael would weigh the evidence against Paul, before pointing an accusing finger at him. This would give her and Justin enough time to reconsider their strategy.

The night before, after she had watched Paul leaving the ruins of the house that had burned down, Gloria had remembered Kenyon's old warning that the killer they were seeking was an artist of strategy. She worried about Lillian. What if he attempted to harm her before anyone had time to prevent him?

"May I make a call from your phone here in the van?"

"Gloria!" By the way Justin said her name she knew he was upset. "Will you at least tell me what you have in mind now?"

"I think Otilia is still at the Cisneros' house. I want to call her. While Paul is busy, we'll be looking in his house for his *treasure*, perhaps find what he's been keeping in whatever it is that he dug up last night."

"Do you really think that Otilia is still going to help you?"

"I'm positive she'll help me, now more than ever. A phone call will prove it," she said to Justin.

Setting up the call for her, Justin handed her the phone. A moment later he heard her say, "Elena, I'd like to talk to Mrs. Juárez." Static answered her plea at the other end, so she told the housekeeper. "I know you can get in trouble with Mr. Cisneros, but it's very important I talk to Otilia. Could you call her to the phone?"

A few seconds later, Otilia answered the phone. "Gloria. Thank God!" she said upon hearing her friend's voice. "I'd been trying to get hold of you all morning. Luisa didn't know where you were. She has gone to the Napa Valley—to Solera—and she asked me to tell you that."

"What?" Gloria exclaimed. Hadn't the doctor told Luisa she shouldn't even drive. Realizing it wasn't the older woman's fault, Gloria tried to soften her tone. "What made Luisa decide to go to the Cisneros' house in the Napa Valley?"

"I asked her to go in my place, so I can go with you to Paul's house later on this afternoon. I don't know what we'll find there, but I think it's important we get to the bottom of this business once and for all. Yet, I didn't want Lilly to be in Oakland where Paul can get to her as easily as he did yesterday. He has a nerve coming in and out of Lilly's house as if it were his own, giving her God-knows-what to drink. And right under my nose!" Otilia sounded quite upset and stopped to catch her breath, then continued, "Lilly begged Michael to let her go to Solera and I backed her up."

Gloria decided to postpone telling Otilia what she and Justin had found at Paul's house, and what had just transpired in Michael's office, until they were on their way to San Francisco.

Instead she asked, "Didn't Michael hire a nurse to take care of Lilly?"

"Yes, he did," Otilia replied. "This nurse he hired is supposed to be a very good nurse, but she has categorically told me she will follow only the doctor's instructions. And this doctor thinks that pumping my daughter full of pills is going to make her well," Otilia continued. "I don't want Lilly to be treated like this, so I told the nurse I was sending Luisa in my place to make sure Lilly doesn't keep taking pills. I'm going to talk to Michael about firing this nurse and consulting an internist."

Even though Gloria was concerned about Luisa's own physical condition, there was little she could do about it now, so she told Otilia she would pick her up in a half hour.

"By the way," Otilia asked, "could you take me to Solera after our visit to Paul's house?"

"Of course, I will," Gloria replied. "I myself was going to suggest that."

Once Otilia reassured her she would be waiting for her, Gloria asked Justin to drop her off at the bus stop, so she could go home to pick up her car.

"Otilia and I are going to Paul's house, then I'm driving her to the Napa Valley, to Solera." Gloria informed Justin.

"Don't you want me to go with you?" he asked.

"No. I know you want to go back to Black Swan to see what the brothers are doing. Right?" He nodded. "We'll have to go our separate ways this time. We have no choice. Is that okay?"

"Agreed."

"Leave a message on my answering machine if there are any complications or anything I should know. I'll check my messages as often as possible."

"Wouldn't it be better if I just meet you later at Solera?" he suggested.

"That's what I had in mind too. There's a restaurant called La Parrilla in Saint Helena. We'll meet there at seven this evening and we'll take it from there."

"Is Solera in Saint Helena?"

"Not quite, but it's just outside town, on Oak Grove Road."

"At seven then," Justin confirmed.

It was twelve when Gloria picked up her car and started up the hill towards the Cisneros' house on Snake Road. Midway up the hill a fine drizzle began to fall. She turned on the radio as Bing Crosby began to sing "White Christmas," one of Darío's favorite Christmas songs, and for a brief moment, she was lost in memories.

Out of nowhere, a doe jumped in front of the car. Gloria swerved and managed to avoid hitting her. The doe quickly disappeared down the slope. In the meantime, Gloria felt her blood rush up and down her temples making her ears buzz. When she regained complete hearing and started uphill again, the song had ended and a steady, whispering rain had begun to fall.

TWENTY-THREE
Mothers, Furies and Fools

Even under normal circumstances, with its two hundred-foot eleva-
tion and its upper and lower levels, each of five lanes, the Oakland-San
Francisco Bay Bridge was a source of anxiety for Gloria. Wind and rain
made her feel particularly apprehensive, and moving in heavy traffic in
those weather conditions sent chills up her spine.

When faced with the first rains, especially after a long dry spell,
drivers often went into some kind of winter madness, and all hell would
break loose on California highways. Already, a produce truck had skid-
ded and turned over as Gloria and Otilia entered the Oakland approach
to the bridge. The only injuries had been half a ton of bleeding tomatoes,
which added to the slickness of the road and forced the closing of three
lanes.

Had it not been for Otilia's inexhaustible serenity, Gloria would have
been a nervous wreck since a trip that would normally have taken forty-
five minutes took them over an hour. They spent the time talking about
the encounter she and Justin had had with Michael that morning, and
about the significance of the photos Justin had gotten from Reyna Galeano
Miller, as well as the unearthing of Paul's mysterious container. They also
discussed ways in which they could keep Lillian under close surveillance.
Gloria volunteered to take a turn watching Lillian that night at Solera and
was almost sure that Justin would take a shift as well.

"That's very nice of you," Otilia sighed. "This has been one sad
Christmas season. It used to be a happy time for Paul and Michael.
Paul would always have family and friends over to celebrate both Christmas and his mother's birthday. If Karen were still alive, she would be
celebrating her eightieth birthday tomorrow."

Gloria felt a tingling just below her ribs—one of the last missing
pieces in the puzzle had just fallen into place. Paul's unearthing of
his box was part of a plan that had been put into motion long ago—

a plan timed to culminate on the anniversary of his mother's birthday. Somehow, Gloria had had this knowledge buried in her psyche and it had driven her daily to the empty lot on Leimert and Monterey during the past two weeks.

Since Black Swan's board meeting was scheduled for the next day, Gloria assumed that Paul's plan had undoubtedly included his taking over the company as interim president. Perhaps he even expected to remain in that position permanently.

Forgetting that Gloria had told her she had already been at Paul's house, Otilia suddenly said, "There it is, the house with the columns. That's Paul's house. Drive up to the front."

"Lee," Otilia addressed the house manager when he opened the door, "I've come to pick up some papers Michael urgently needs. May we come in? Paul said they're most likely on his desk." Lee was quite pleased to see Otilia, but seemed to question Gloria's presence there. "This is Mrs. Damasco, a friend of my daughter's," Otilia said, putting her arm around Gloria's shoulder. "She has been kind enough to drive me here. You wouldn't believe the madness on that bridge."

At that point, Lee greeted both women with a cordial smile. "I believe you, Mrs. Juárez. It is worse every year, especially around this time of year. Christmas madness!" he said with a slight southern drawl. "Please let me show you," he added, as he led them to Paul's study, "where the papers are supposed to be." He left the door open, but permitted them to look for themselves.

Gloria was amazed at how easy it had been to penetrate Paul's inner sanctum. Unlike the feelings she had had when she and Justin had come into the house the night before, this time she had no extra-sensory perception about this situation.

Both women began by looking for the small box that Justin had told Gloria he had seen the night before and for the mysterious cylinder. But neither of the containers was there. They did find the other two safes in Paul's study, but without the lock combination these were inaccessible to them. Otilia told Gloria to wait in the study while she went up to Paul's bedroom to look for the combination.

While she waited, Gloria checked the papers stacked on a work table next to the computer. Seeing part of a hand printed on the edge of a slip of paper barely showing under a paperweight, she lifted the weight. The *Irmandade*'s emblem became fully visible. Under the emblem someone had noted, "BSI Fin. data. Anac. Inter." Another line read, "Varig 156 SFO 3:00 12–16." Someone from Anaconda Sur International was leaving or arriving at the San Francisco Airport that day, December 16, to get financial data about Black Swan.

Before going upstairs after Otilia, Gloria swiftly rummaged through the papers on the desk and in its drawers, but found mostly sales sheets, graphs and other financial data concerning Black Swan. She took a few of the sales graphs and put them in a folder, in case Lee wondered about the papers Otilia had come to get. Then her eye caught the red-green edge of a seal on a yellowing envelope that stuck out of a legal size, unmarked manila folder. She pulled it out to half of its length. Visible on the upper left hand corner, under the red and green colors of the Mexican flag, was an eagle standing on a cactus, devouring a serpent—the official seal of Mexico. Gloria retrieved the envelope quickly and put it in her purse, then went out into the hall. Since Lee didn't seem to be anywhere in sight, she headed upstairs and into the master bedroom after Otilia. She found Otilia just as she was coming out of the bathroom that opened to the master bedroom. They startled each other.

"I found something," Gloria whispered. "Let's go."

As she began to walk towards the door of the bedroom, Gloria glanced at the night table. Her heart jolted when she saw that the Smith and Wesson .357 which had been there the night before was now missing. Otilia's voice prompted her to keep moving, for they could hear Lee talking to someone in the kitchen. There was a pause in the conversation followed by the creaking of the service stairs. Quietly, Gloria and Otilia moved down the front stairs and waited for Lee, who met them a moment later at the door, then stood in the driveway until they drove away.

Driving to the first available pay phone, Gloria was able to reach Justin in his van. She informed him of the meeting that was about to take place at the airport. Justin told her he was already following Paul and briefly reported that Michael had been going about his business as usual. He had apparently not said anything to Paul about their visit to his office that morning.

When Gloria went back to the car, Otilia had already taken the papers out of the envelope Gloria had found. Placing them on her lap one by one, she had carefully read them. The first thing she pulled out were adoption papers for a three day-old infant boy, born in the *Hospital de Beneficencia General de México*, to Celia C. de Peralta. The second item was a certificate of baptism registered at the *Basílica de la Virgen de Guadalupe* four days after the birth of the child, who, according to the certificate, had been given the name of Michael Cisneros, Jr. The certificate also stated that Michael Sr. and his wife were the natural parents of the child. Next was the registration of Michael Jr. as a citizen of the United States of America by virtue of his parentage, witnessed and notarized by officials of the American Embassy in Mexico City.

"I know the evidence is staring at us now from all sides, but I still can't understand what causes Paul to behave like this," Gloria complained. "What moves him?"

"Since our talk about Paul's actions yesterday, I've been giving a great deal of thought to this business of Michael's adoption and Paul's attitude towards him and Lilly." Otilia paused to collect her thoughts. "No matter how I look at this dreadful business, I seem to always go in circles. I keep coming back to old Mr. Bjorgun. I keep thinking about that fight between Michael Sr. and Karen's father, how he tried to blame Michael Sr. for his own bad relationship with her.

"Then, I recall how a few months later, Mr. Bjorgun fell gravely ill and asked that Paul remain at his bedside. By that time, Michael Sr. was also ill. A few weeks after his grandfather Bjorgun passed away, Paul returned home a very rich young man because his grandfather had bequeathed to him half of his fortune. Nevertheless, Paul was moody and despondent. I suppose everyone accepted this kind of behavior knowing he and his grandfather had been very close.

"For a while after his return, Paul continued to be irascible and prone to fits of unexplained anger, and on occasion, he even became abusive towards his father. On several occasions, Michael had to intervene and physically restrain Paul. Everyone thought he would get over that phase of displaced grief. Eventually he did, of course. But now ... "

"Now, you think that he never really did get over his anger," Gloria offered, as they entered the highway on their way to the wine country.

"I'm not sure any more what I really think about this terrible business." Otilia sounded tired.

Gloria saw the slight trembling of Otilia's hands—no doubt the result of a most stressful day and the cold weather. She turned up the heater in the car for the older woman's comfort. This must have made Otilia drowsy, for the next time Gloria looked in her direction, her head was bobbing. Reaching out to the older woman, Gloria pushed her gently so Otilia could rest her head on the seat. Seeing Otilia fast asleep, Gloria thought of her own mother, whom she hadn't seen for a few days.

Then, her thoughts drifted over the many mothers who had been involved in this case. Lillian Cisneros and Mando's mother, Flora Cadena, had certainly suffered the greatest losses. Then, there were Cecilia Castro-Biddle and Karen Bjorgun-Cisneros, who had unwittingly unleashed furies and fools on the rest of them. They seemed to be caught in a game where all the main players were men, and the losers were all women and their children. When this was over—as in time of war and subsequent peace—the women would have to swallow their grief and their shame. They would have to comfort and support each other, then begin the long and painful task of rebuilding their lives.

TWENTY-FOUR
Fantasies for Tolerable Tomorrows

After Gloria dropped Otilia off at Solera, she and Luisa headed towards La Parrilla Restaurant to talk with Justin. During dinner, he told them that Paul had met with two other men in the cocktail lounge at the airport's international terminal. One was dressed in a suit and tie; the other was younger and wore more casual clothes. The younger man moved to another table after he exchanged greetings with Paul.

Justin could not hear what Paul and the man in the suit talked about, but he had noticed that both Paul and the older man were wearing a ring with a lion's head. After a brief conversation, Paul handed the older man a thick manila envelope containing, in all likelihood, the data about Black Swan's financial status for Anaconda Sur International. From the airport, Paul had gone back to Michael's house on Snake Road in Oakland.

After dinner, Luisa, Gloria and Justin headed back to Solera. As soon as the rain stopped, fog descended on the wine country, and transit through the narrow, dimly-lit roads in the valley, with only a twenty-foot visibility, had become quite dangerous.

As a young woman, Gloria had considered fog a negative element, a symbol of apathy and blindness. Then, as time passed, she became aware of her preference for misty days and even looked forward to clouds descending on the Bay Area like children on a playground. Then, fog afforded her the opportunity, in Luisa's words, "of finding the finest memory, the softest music, the fantasy that would make exciting any barely tolerable tomorrow."

Tonight, however, Gloria wished for a clear night. As they entered the driveway, Justin parted company with the two women and began to look for a strategic spot to park his van. He gave Gloria a walkie-talkie to use only in an emergency.

After a brief chat, Luisa and Otilia went to bed while Gloria took a seat by the window in her room to wait out the night. Somewhere out there, she thought, surrounded by the heavy mist, Justin's van was parked. Even though it was equipped with a cassette player, books, and a TV, he could probably not do much of anything for fear someone might spot him. So by now, he was probably sitting in it, quietly, rubbing his arms and legs to keep warm, sipping coffee, stretching every so often to keep from falling asleep. A private detective had to be able to entertain himself with his own imagination—or else have none whatsoever—to withstand nights like this one, with no more company than darkness and mist, waiting for death to show its hand.

Gloria longed to be out there, too, talking with Justin instead of looking out the window and hearing the creaking of beds as people turned in their sleep. The walkie-talkie in her hand would not be really handy in communicating with Justin unless something important came up. The static and the noise might be heard by anyone in the house or anyone eaves-dropping out there.

Suddenly Gloria was aware of the sound of music and singing coming from far away. She pressed the button of her walkie-talkie and spoke very softly. "Justin, I think someone's singing. It may be Lillian. I'm going to check this out." She went out of the dark room into a darker hallway and began to walk towards the living and dining areas. The singing— definitely from *Madame Butterfly*—stopped as Gloria approached the living room. Accustomed to the darkness by now, she looked around the room but couldn't see anyone there.

Remembering that the winery offices and the tasting and sales room were across the courtyard, Gloria walked into the kitchen and looked out the window into the yard. But visibility, even with the yellow floodlights, was only about ten feet in any direction, not enough for her to see what was happening in the winery offices.

On the way back to her room, Gloria put her ear on Lillian's door. At first she couldn't hear anything other than the nurse's snores. Then, as she opened the door, she heard the first line of "Un bel di." The music was coming from inside the room and Gloria looked for its source, concluding after a brief search that it was coming from a cassette player underneath Lillian's pillow. Feeling carefully for the button, she turned off the music. Lillian immediately moaned and turned over, but went back to sleep.

All the time that Gloria had been in the room, the nurse hadn't moved even once; and Gloria was certain that if Lillian were to leave the room, the nurse wouldn't notice.

"Everything's fine," Gloria told Justin after she was back in her room.

"Okay," his voice said at the other end.

With her eyes closed, she sat by the window and let her mind drift.

But a short time later, she realized she had actually been hearing Lillian's sobbing and pleading voice for some time.

She started down the hall again, pushing towards the place from where the sobbing came. In her haste, she dropped the walkie-talkie. Swearing under her breath, she picked it up and looked around. Cautiously, she pressed and released the button twice. Justin had circled around the winery to check on some noise he had been hearing and didn't respond to Gloria's signal.

The house was quiet, and outside, the night was dense and dark. Then suddenly, as Gloria entered the kitchen, she was aware of another presence nearby. The shadow of a man moved through the courtyard. Gloria retreated past the living room to the hall and, pressing the button of the walkie-talkie, she spoke softly into it. "Justin, didn't you say Paul was in Oakland? I think I just saw him in the courtyard." For a second time, Justin didn't answer.

Suddenly, the sound of soft steps behind her made her turn around quickly. Brandishing the walkie-talkie as a weapon, she got ready to face Paul. Instead, she saw a groggy Luisa step out of the darkness of the hall in a Mexican-pink satin nightgown.

"Please go back to sleep," Gloria begged, but Luisa wouldn't hear of it. "At least go put on my robe," Gloria relented.

"Where are we going?" Luisa asked when she rejoined her friend.

"Don't know exactly. Paul's here. I know it." Gloria felt Luisa's very cold hand on her arm, and shivered. "You're cutting the circulation off in your hand. Release the bandage."

Luisa laughed softly. "That was my *good* hand ... "

The sound of Lillian's sobbing was definitely coming from somewhere around the kitchen, and Gloria and Luisa began to walk in that direction. The crying suddenly stopped. A minute later they heard it again, but Lillian's pleading voice seemed to be coming from farther away. Gloria and Luisa started up again. At about the point where the living room and dining room met, they heard Lillian murmur, "*M'ijito. I'm coming.*"

"*La llorona,*" whispered Luisa as her trembling hand squeezed Gloria's arm, "It's spooky."

Luisa and Gloria heard Lillian's cry once again as they approached the kitchen. Through the window they caught sight of Lillian in her nightgown, just as she stepped out into the dark and misty yard. Instinctively Luisa grabbed hold of Gloria's arm. In spite of their apprehension, they followed Lillian outside.

As Gloria began to walk on the wet, cold grass, she looked down at her shoes but she couldn't see them. Immediately she realized that someone had turned off the floodlights. Moving blindly in the misty darkness, she felt cut off from the source of her psychic energy and lost contact with Luisa who had gone ahead. "Luisa," Gloria whispered. No one answered. She panicked. Then, she heard someone say, "I'm sorry." She reached into the misty space, but her hand came up empty.

A hand grabbed her by the arm while another covered her mouth. Then someone whispered very close to her ear, "Sh! It's okay. It's me."

Gloria was furious, not at Justin but at herself for letting fear take control of her. Pulling her arm free from his grip, she asked, "Where have you been? I've been signaling you."

"I know." He began to tug at her. Pointing her finger in the direction of the office, he put his arm around her shoulder to guide her. "Over there ... the winery offices." Shivering, Gloria felt the warmth of his breath just above her hair and instinctively huddled closer to him. With her hand she reached across his back to hold herself up.

At that moment, Luisa stepped out of the fog and almost bumped into them. "They are there," she said, then clarified, "Paul and Lillian are in the sales room. He seems to have her under his control. She looks awful."

The three of them began to walk faster, heading towards the sliding door in the tasting room. The yellow night lamps on both sides of the door provided enough light for them to see where they were going.

Gloria flashed back to the night, eighteen years before, when she and Luisa had also crouched in the dark, waiting for Mando. Even though she no longer felt responsible for his death, she had promised herself then that she would never risk anyone's life again. Yet, once more, here she was, putting Justin and Luisa in danger. She glanced at her friend, whose face looked drawn and pale. Although Luisa was breathing hard, she showed no uncertainty in her eyes as the two friends heard Lillian's voice.

"I want to die," Lillian was saying, in a listless way. "I want to die."

"You can't die. Not yet." Paul's voice was cold. "You have to write your farewell note to Michael, remember?"

"Farewell note to Michael? What do I say to Michael?" A whimper started to come out of her. "Please help me die. I want to die," she whispered.

"Yes, I'll help you, but first the note," Paul demanded, and Gloria could hear the rustle of pages. "Tell him that you have always loved me," he commanded. "Say that you have decided you can no longer face life without me."

"Why would I tell Michael that?" Lillian's speech was slurred and Gloria began to suspect that Lillian had taken a few tranquilizers. "I don't love you," Lillian continued. "I have always, always hated you. Ever since—since—that night."

"Yes. Our night together. Twenty-two years ago." There wasn't a trace of irony in Paul's voice and the coldness had suddenly turned to sweetness.

"The tenderness of the *snake*," Luisa whispered in a raspy voice.

Putting her index finger over her lips, Gloria asked Luisa to keep quiet as she caught Justin's shadow out of the corner of her eye, moving towards the door. Then she saw him exit quietly.

With her shoulder gently resting on the wall to keep her balance, she began to inch her way closer to the door. Luisa was right behind her, breathing hard. They heard Paul's voice closer to them. "All right, my love, sit here and write your farewell."

Silence.

"You were lovely that night, too," Paul continued. "I still remember your beautiful hair. Your round breasts. And the strength with which you fought."

The doorway was only a few inches away and Gloria began to bend slowly to gain a better view. Paul was pouring the elixir from a bottle similar to the one Gloria and Justin had found in Paul's home. Her heart began to race.

Paul continued in an angry tone. "But I had to give you away to *him*, the bastard who took away everything I loved. Grandfather was right. 'Take back what is yours to begin with,' he told me. 'Make him suffer. Make him pay.' 'Yes,' I promised Grandfather. And I've kept my promise. I have waited so long for this. But it will be over soon, my love. Drink this. It will make you feel better."

Suddenly, a shadow moved past one of the windows. Gloria recognized Justin. His curly hair and his profile were unmistakable.

Paul had his back to the windows and to the door. A desk lamp on the other side of the bar directed light on Lillian. She was sitting on the counter with a wine glass in her hand full of the opaque liquid while Paul stood next to her. The amount in the glass was four times what he had given Lillian to drink the day before. Even half of what was in the glass, combined with the tranquilizers, would prove lethal.

A large oak-framed mirror hung above the bar. Reflected on it Gloria's eyes caught a dark object half hidden under the pad Paul had brought for Lillian's farewell note to Michael.

"Drink up, my Little Butterfly. Drink up." He removed a strand of hair from her face and began to hum "Un bel di." She looked at him as if she were in a trance. Slowly she began to raise the glass to her lips. He caressed her cheek.

It was difficult to tell from a distance, but Gloria thought she saw tears in Paul's eyes. Then, he said softly, "I have never wanted to hurt you, but Michael David was *his* son and I ... I was bound by my honor to kill ... "

Lillian had almost put the glass to her lips, but as soon as she heard Paul's words, she stood up and threw the contents of the glass at Paul. "You, bastard! You, fool!" Clutching her stomach, she went down on her knees, laughing hysterically. "Don't you see? Didn't you ever wonder why I couldn't have any more children?" She rocked lightly, still pressing on her stomach. All of a sudden she was on her feet. "Michael David was *your* son!" Her hands began to tear at Paul's face. "He was your son! And you killed him!"

For an instant, Paul was paralyzed. Then, his eyes moved in all directions. As he let go of the pad, Gloria saw the gun in his hand. Then Lillian sprang forward to attack him. He stretched out his other hand and caught her by the throat. Unable to just stand there without doing anything, Gloria burst into the tasting room and began to circle towards the sliding door.

"Don't be a fool, Gloria," Luisa said with a quavering voice. "He has a gun."

Gloria took two deep breaths, then moved forward a few steps, but stayed in the semi-darkness. "What are you doing with that gun, Paul? Give it to me. You can hurt yourself." Paul heard enough authority in her voice to hesitate for an instant.

Without moving, she took another deep breath and said in a gentler tone. "And I would be so unhappy if anything happened to my beautiful blond boy." Surprised, Paul let go of Lillian. She collapsed to the floor unconscious.

Luisa cleared her throat, but all she managed to say was "Otilia ... " before Paul began to move towards Gloria. She stood her ground. Luisa moved closer to her. Paul stopped. He blinked a few times, and Gloria knew the spell had been broken. Now he was coming at her, no longer as if to embrace his mother, but to make her pay the debt she owed him.

A shadow reflected on the mirror as someone approached the sliding door. The noise of a car was audible in the distance. In a matter of seconds the vehicle came to a screeching halt. "Michael," Luisa said, but it sounded more like a question. Gloria heard someone running in their direction at the same time the safety of a gun was being released. Luisa and Gloria turned just as Paul leaped forward, intending to wrap his arm around Gloria's neck. Luisa grabbed at him to keep him from choking her friend. Paul pushed Luisa away and she staggered backwards.

"Let her go," they heard someone say. Then, they all realized it was Otilia who was aiming Paul's Smith and Wesson at him with both her hands. Gloria had never seen such hatred in Otilia's eyes, but the older woman's hands shook so badly Gloria doubted that Otilia could aim accurately or even pull the trigger for that matter. At that instant, another shadow moved towards Otilia and she took a step back. Had Michael finally shown up, Gloria wondered, as she felt Paul relax his lock on her.

Paul laughed softly, almost like a naughty child at play. "Welcome, dear *brother*. Join the party," he said, as a hand reached out from the darkness and took the gun from Otilia's hand. Michael then came into view. His hand was steady but he couldn't quite size up what was happening.

Paul locked his arm tighter around Gloria's neck. Her chest heaved for breath. Not wanting to abandon herself to death so easily, she made one last effort to save herself and she unexpectedly let her body go limp. This gave her the chance to rotate within Paul's grip, forcing him to release her so he could pull her up to him again. She turned a second time, and pushed him away as hard as she could. He reeled over. She looked up at the mirror as Justin suddenly opened the sliding door, lunged into the room and rolled over, with his gun pointing at them at all times.

Paul began to move towards Gloria again. His face was pale and almost unrecognizable. His mouth twitched a little as if he were trying to contain a scream. Luisa also moved in Gloria's direction. As Luisa's hand pushed her out of Paul's way, Gloria tumbled forward. At that moment Paul pulled the trigger. The sound deafened her. Luisa gasped, put her hand to the side of her neck, and fell to her knees. Gloria tried to reassure her friend that she herself was all right, but she seemed incapable of articulating any sounds.

Out of the corner of her eye, Gloria saw the sparks coming from Justin's gun as he too pulled the trigger. She was unable to hear anything, but she did get a quick glance at the stunned look in Paul's eyes as he keeled over and fell on the floor next to her. Then, Gloria felt the weight of Luisa's head on her chest and heard a gurgling sound as a warm liquid spread all over her chest and stomach. Freeing her arm, she passed it around Luisa's back and heard her friend take a deep breath only to let it out so slowly that the exhalation seemed endless. She couldn't tell who it was that whispered in her ear, "I'm sorry, Gloria," as a warm gust of blue light brushed against her cheek.

TWENTY-FIVE

A Murderer's Treasure Box

There's something comforting in the inalterable cycles of nature, Luisa had said once as she and Gloria watched some geysers, propelled by their own steam, shoot up and show their rainbows on contact with morning's first light. Now, Luisa was gone and Gloria could hardly conceive of her life without her friend's love and constant presence.

After Paul's and Luisa's bodies were removed from the winery, the sheriff permitted Michael and Otilia to visit Lillian at the hospital where she had been taken. Justin and Gloria were asked to go to the sheriff's office for questioning. There, they waited for Sheriff Parnell while the deputies finished transcribing their depositions, so the two could sign them.

"Please," she vaguely heard Justin say to the sheriff's deputy who had been questioning them. "I know as much about this as anyone else. I pulled the trigger. Let Mrs. Damasco go home."

Gloria wanted to tell Justin not to insist on her going home, that Oakland seemed to be a million miles away, and that she preferred to stay there with him. But since she had been given a sedative, she barely could hold a thought, let alone articulate it. Her mind and body were still trapped in the state which precedes grief.

Despite the sedative, the certainty that she was responsible for her best friend's death sat on her chest like a rock, allowing her only shallow breathing and almost no feeling. She remembered what her grandmother used to tell her, *"No te tragues las lágrimas*—Don't swallow your tears. Let them out. If you swallow them, they'll multiply inside you. And one day you'll cry an ocean and *it* will swallow *you."*

Remembering Lillian and her pool of tears, Gloria thought that perhaps there was still some hope for Lillian. Was there any hope for herself, she wondered.

An hour later, having left Lillian resting comfortably at the hospital,

Michael and Otilia entered the sheriff's office and found Gloria and Justin still there.

Michael shook Justin's hand, asking him in a low voice, "Are the deputies giving you a hard time?"

"Not more than expected." Justin took a deep breath to ease the anxiety he felt, as he recalled that only a few hours earlier he had fatally shot Paul Cisneros.

Michael turned to Gloria. He held her hand and patted it gently while he said, "Mrs. Damasco, I can't begin to tell you how sorry I am about all this." His voice quavered, as he continued, "I wish I could turn the clock back ... Mrs. Juárez and my wife and I are forever in your debt." His hand started shaking and he withdrew it. Gloria nodded.

Then, Otilia sat beside Gloria, making her younger friend lean on her shoulder as she said, "I'm so sorry, my dear. So very sorry." Smoothing Gloria's hair with her fingers, she spoke softly to her, "I called your mother like you asked me to. She and Luisa's mother are already heading this way. Tania is driving them here. Michael wants Mrs. Cortez and you to know that he will take care of all funeral expenses."

Gloria wanted to thank Otilia and Michael for their offer, but her mouth didn't seem to obey her.

Turning to the deputy, Michael asked, "Why is Mrs. Damasco still here?" Speaking with authority, he added, "Mrs. Damasco just lost her best friend. She doesn't know any more than Mr. Escobar and I do."

Knowing that Michael was a winery owner in the valley, the deputy was more responsive to him than to Justin. "All right, Mr. Cisneros. She can go as soon as she signs the deposition."

The deputy turned to Justin. "Not you. You better stick around. There are a lot of questions the sheriff will want to ask you."

At that moment, Michael's chauffeur entered, carrying a cardboard box. He set it on the table, then left.

"My corroboration of the facts might expedite this matter." Michael pointed to the tape recorder on the desk, then sat down. "Why don't we go on with it? When the sheriff comes you'll have it all together for him."

The deputy agreed and switched on the tape recorder. Justin sat next to Gloria as Michael began to talk.

"Eighteen years ago my son was killed in East Los Angeles. Michael David was only four years old at the time of his death. All these years, the case had remained unsolved," Michael said as he reached into the box his chauffeur had brought in. "Mr. Escobar and Mrs. Damasco walked into my office yesterday morning with this package." He took out the large manila envelope with copies of Gloria's notes and clippings, and of Kenyon's files. Then he brought out the photo carrier with the enlargements of Joel Galeano's photos.

Sheriff Parnell walked into the office. "We can dispense with all that, Mr. Cisneros," he said as he walked to the coat rack and hung his hat. "I know it's still very painful for you and we have all the details Mrs. Damasco and Escobar here have given us about your son's death."

"Very well. Thank you," Michael said and he reached into the cardboard box again. He looked like a weary magician, Gloria thought, reaching in for doves and pulling snakes out of a hat, as he took out a small metal box that turned out to be the same one Michael Sr. had used to keep his personal papers. Otilia had mentioned that particular box to Gloria many years before, adding that Michael had referred to it as one of Paul's treasure boxes. Justin looked at Gloria and nodded, indicating it was the same small metal file he'd seen at Paul's house two nights before.

Gloria felt a part of herself begin to come alive again as Michael continued to provide answers to the many questions she had had about the case. Greater than her curiosity, she knew, was her need to restore the order that had been upset by Luisa's death.

The sheriff opened the box and took out its contents. An odd assortment it was. First, he came up with a photo of Paul as a child, holding a pet rabbit.

"Was this your brother's favorite pet?" Gloria asked Michael, recalling her vision at Paul's house.

"Yes, it was," Michael answered. "Paul loved that rabbit so much. He would take his pet to bed with him. He'd imitate the rabbit, munching on carrots and lettuce and hopping around the house."

At first a hint of amusement surfaced in Michael's gaze as he drifted into this memory of childhood. But soon he turned serious again as he recalled Paul's deeds. "As children, we can be so unkind ... " Michael prefaced what he was about to say. "I loved Paul very much, yet ... Well, at that time, I remember telling him that if he loved his rabbit so much, he would not mind eating the rabbit's ... droppings. With childish bravado, Paul said he could eat them but at the last minute he backed down. I didn't mean to be cruel towards Paul, but I'm afraid I was, for one day I put a couple of the rabbit's droppings in his cocoa. When he saw them at the bottom of the glass, Paul couldn't finish his drink. He was so angry that he started after me, armed with a table knife. Mother punished him for doing that, but she didn't punish me for my nasty prank.

"My brother was so upset that he stopped looking after his pet. I felt ashamed and began to feed his rabbit myself. Actually, I too grew very fond of that little rabbit. Paul would watch me play with it from afar. Then, one day, we got home from school and Mother told us that she had found our pet floating in the swimming pool. Somehow he had drowned. Paul was very upset and kept blaming Mother, then me, for the death of his rabbit." He paused. "Even Grandfather Bjorgun came to scold me for not looking after the pet," he continued. "My mother immediately came to my defense. I had no idea that the rabbit's death would be the start of Paul's hatred towards me." Michael's voice quavered and he paused again to regain his composure. Then he added, "I had no idea his hatred would make my brother one day fill my son's mouth with his own ... " But he could not complete the thought.

Otilia reached out and squeezed Michael's hand.

When Gloria heard Michael imply that Paul had put the excrement in little Michael's mouth, she thought at first she had not heard right. A silly childhood prank hardly seemed to her reason enough for anyone to fill an innocent child's mouth with excrement. But when she glanced at Justin, his eyes confirmed she had fully understood what Michael said. She couldn't bring herself to ask Michael any more questions.

At that moment, the sheriff picked up an old pistol from among the contents of the box, and said, "Military issue, World War II."

Justin decided to wait for another opportunity to find out what else Michael knew about his son's murder.

The sheriff began to study the rest of the contents in the box: rocks and crystals, and two beautiful yellow tail butterflies in wooden frames. There were also many family photos, including a picture of Lillian and Michael on their wedding day.

Michael glanced at Gloria as she looked at the many photos of his mother Karen either holding or hugging him. Only one of the photos showed Karen holding Paul as a baby.

Michael took a deep breath, letting it out slowly. Somewhat eased, he returned to his story. "My brother always felt that I was mother's favorite. But that wasn't the case, even though it is true that she and I got along well. Paul resented that she seemed to enjoy my company more than his. You see, I was physically so unlike her, he reasoned that he should be favored by our mother because he looks ... looked so much like her—like Grandfather Bjorgun—blonde and tall, with grayish blue eyes ... Paul wanted so much to belong, so much for people to approve of him.

"When Paul was eight years old, he came home one day after school and went directly to the bathroom. I found him scrubbing his face with a soapy bristle hairbrush, so hard that his cheek was beginning to bleed. I made him stop the scrubbing but he cried and cried. Mother was very concerned but she didn't ask him why he had hurt himself. She just put some antibiotic remedy on his face and took him to the doctor the next day. But I did ask my brother why he'd acted as he had.

"At the time, we were both attending a rather exclusive private school, where only a handful of children—including Paul and me—were of non-European extraction. The kids at school, Paul said, had laughed at him. They had taunted him, telling him that under his white skin, he was brown like Father and me. When our parents found out about that, they went to the school to complain. They even wanted to transfer us to another school. But Paul was even more upset at this. Then—you see— our schoolmates might think that he was running away because he was really brown underneath. I tried to console him, to tell him it wasn't important ... "

Justin snorted. "I thought that happened only to us, poor Chicano kids in the barrios," he said bitterly. "You were—are rich. I thought that money recognized no other color but green."

"To some extent you're right. But, had Paul been an only child, with his looks, his predicament wouldn't have existed. But I, his older brother, gave him away every time. In a way, I must admit I too have succumbed to this way of thinking. In our company, I let Paul take care of public relations, I let him deal with our clients." Michael's tone was becoming angry. "I was willing to run things behind the scene."

Well aware of the scenario Michael was describing, Justin lowered his eyes and kept quiet. Michael turned his attention to the sheriff, who had reached into a small cylinder and was now emptying its contents on the table.

Sheriff Parnell held up a silk-screened cloth with the emblem of the Brazilian brotherhood—the *Irmandade*. The emblem was also engraved in gold leaf on the soft leather covers of two books, one bearing the name of Michael Cisneros Belho—Justin and Gloria surmised that Michael Sr. had used his mother's maiden name, as is the Latin American custom. The other book bore the name of Paul C. Bjorgun-Smith.

Sheriff Parnell began to peruse a thin roll of computer data sheets, also exhibiting the emblem of the brotherhood, then he picked up Michael Sr.'s book and opened it. Skimming over a few pages, he asked, "Mr. Cisneros, how did you come across these books?" Throwing a quick glance at Michael, he continued his perusal of the book.

"Yesterday afternoon, before I decided to come to Solera," Michael explained, "my brother and I finished preparing our reports for the company's board meeting. He said goodbye and I assumed he had gone to his house in San Francisco."

"But he hadn't?" Sheriff Parnell asked.

Michael shook his head by way of an answer. "Yesterday morning, Mr. Escobar and Mrs. Damasco left all this material at my office," Michael said, pointing at the enlargements and at Gloria's and Kenyon's files. "I had asked my chauffeur to put everything in a box to take to my house in Oakland," he continued. "So after my brother left, I looked through the box. Not daring to believe that my brother could be capable of such violence, I called his home, hoping he would be able to explain his actions. His house manager told me that Paul had not gotten home yet. Unable to decide on a course of action, I called my wife at Solera and tried to talk to her, but she was beyond reasoning.

"Hoping perhaps that Mr. Escobar and Mrs. Damasco were wrong, I again looked at the enlargement of the ring with a lion's head that had belonged to my father. I made up my mind then to go to my brother's house. At first, I primarily wanted to understand why he too would join an organization like the *Irmandade*, a kind of army, so to speak. Paul had a gun collection, yet, he had never shown any preference for the military. He wasn't drafted during the war in Vietnam, and he wouldn't have volunteered for any active military duty or reserve, for that matter. I felt burdened realizing I didn't know this man I called my brother. I made up my mind to confront Paul, but he still wasn't home. There, I found this box and the cylinder."

"I think your brother unearthed the cylinder the night before last," Justin explained. "He had it buried in the lot at Leimert and Monterey."

Michael cleared his throat. "I think the *Irmandade* may be up to something. To tell you all the truth, at Black Swan we've been under a threat of a takeover by a larger conglomerate, which is primarily backed by foreign investors. But since Paul and I are—were—the major stockholders, I never took these threats seriously. Yesterday morning, at my office, when Mrs. Damasco pointed out the possibility that Paul had succeeded in pushing me out of Black Swan, I began to suspect there might be something I was overlooking. Then, in the late afternoon yesterday, when I got to Paul's house, I began to study the ledgers and data of the *Irmandade*, and I became aware that indeed there would be a takeover, and that Paul was behind it."

"Can you give us a summary of what we'll find in these?" Sheriff Parnell fanned the pages of Michael Sr.'s book, then put his hand on Paul's book, and on the ledgers and data sheets.

"Yes. The book you're holding is a field journal I've read often. It was kept by my father when he was a member of the *Irmandade*. The organization was founded before World War II by my grandfather, Soren Bjorgun, together with six other industrialists from Argentina, Brazil, Mexico, England, Germany and the U.S. Their goal was to fund a number of small "intelligence" groups in several Latin American countries. These were not diminutive CIA's. In fact, they had nothing to do with any government operation. I suppose the best way to describe them is as socio-financial 'think tanks.'

"The *Irmandade* members thought of ways to increase the productivity of smaller companies. They provided their expertise and some resources and funds for expansion or diversification once those companies had a solid financial base. The smaller companies repaid their benefactors simply by making it possible for them to open up new markets for their products.

"Then, war broke out in Europe and the German members of the *Irmandade* moved their operations out of Germany into Brazil, Argentina and Mexico, relocating again after the war was over. But by that time, new elements in the think tanks began to change the nature and direction of the *Irmandade*.

"My father had always wanted to be president of the *Irmandade*, but my grandfather had opposed his appointment."

"Your father and grandfather didn't get along, is that what you're saying, Mr. Cisneros?"

"Yes. Grandfather Bjorgun was a very difficult man, and he had only tolerated my father because he would have lost my mother altogether if he hadn't. At my mother's insistance, my grandfather even made it possible for my father to acquire two steel mills in Oakland. Then, in 1957, despite my grandfather's efforts to the contrary, my father became president of the organization.

"My father was actually the last president of the old *Irmandade*. Due to all the unrest in the Latin American countries, the founding members, with the exception of Grandfather Bjorgun, who decided to start a whole new group, voted with my father to disband the groups."

"What year was that, Mr. Cisneros?" The sheriff asked.

"That was 1960. My grandfather died a few months after that, and my father passed away in '67. I had assumed my family's connections to the *Irmandade* had ended at that point."

"But that's when your brother became involved in the organization, wasn't it?" the sheriff asked. "That's what these dates after your brother's name mean. *That* is your brother's name, isn't it?" He looked at Michael, who nodded. "Do you know why he used the initical 'C' and this other name, 'Bjorgun-Smith'?"

"The hyphenated last name was my mother's. You must understand
that Paul and our grandfather Soren Bjorgun were very close. For many
years as a baby and later as a young man, Paul literally lived with the
Bjorgun-Smiths. Late yesterday afternoon as I read my brother's journal,
I discovered that for all intents and purposes, he considered grandfather
his *true* father. Soren Bjorgun resented my father almost to the point
of hatred, and he thoroughly disliked me as well. Paul mentions that
Grandfather Bjorgun loved him so much that when I was four years
old, he even attempted to have me kidnapped by my own ... biological
mother. In that way, Paul, who had just been born, would remain as
sole heir." Michael's voice caught in his throat, but he went on. "Many
years later, father wound up making me the president of the company.
Yet, I was the bastard—the illegitimate—in Soren Bjorgun's eyes and
consequently in Paul's eyes as well. I'm not sure whether the old man
intended all this to happen as it did, but Paul—and even my own son
Michael David—were, in the end, grandfather's victim." Michael fell
silent.

"Are you saying that in some distorted way your brother had your
son killed to please Soren Bjorgun?" the sheriff asked.

"I'm afraid so," Michael breathed deeply, then continued. "In entry
after entry in that journal he wrote of his hatred for me and our mother
because of her love for me."

"And he used the means available to him through this new *Irmandade*?" the sheriff inquired.

"Yes, it's all in Paul's field journal," Michael stated. "He and three
others—sons of the European founders—re-established it, but the orga-
nizational goals were no longer those the founding members had sought
to achieve. Under the new leadership, the *Irmandade* began to function
more like a military hierarchy. They recruited people like Joel Galeano to
do their dirty work. Paul and the other leaders were the 'intelligentsia'—
each a combination of field-commander and strategist."

Sheriff Parnell raised his eyebrows. "Are all the names here?"

Michael shook his head. "My brother wasn't so foolish as to write
down real names. I'm sure they're all code names for people and cities.
But the F.B.I. shouldn't have any trouble decoding it." Michael placed
his hand on his father's field journal, then withdrew it immediately.

"Mr. Cisneros," Justin said, "excuse the question, but do you think
that Paul personally killed your son or do you think he had someone else
kill him?"

There was a long pause before Michael responded. "I'm quite sure

Paul personally killed Michael David."

"Earlier you mentioned that Paul had filled your son's mouth with
... " Justin paused to take a deep breath.

"Excrement." Michael's lips trembled, nevertheless he completed
Justin's statement, and added, "Paul mentions that in his journal, but he
didn't provide an explanation. I didn't have any inkling as to what his
motive might be until I saw the photo of Paul holding his rabbit and I
remembered the stupid prank I played on him," Michael concluded. "No
matter how hard I try I cannot find any other credible explanation for
Paul's desire to defile my son's body."

"How was he able to kill Michael David, Mr. Cisneros?" Justin asked,
pointing at the field journal. "He was supposed to be in Bavaria, wasn't
he?"

Taking a small manila envelope out of the box, Michael emptied its
contents on the desk. The sheriff searched through them. In addition
to a passport in the name of Paul Smith, there was a receipt for a round
trip from Frankfurt to Los Angeles. Paul had obviously arrived in Los
Angeles at noon on Saturday, August 29, 1970, and had boarded the
night flight back to Frankfurt that very same day.

"As I just finished reading here in your brother's journal," the sheriff stated, "he had a woman—a Cecilia Castro-Biddle—abduct Michael
David from Mrs. Juárez's house. This woman enticed your son out of
the house by showing him a big Mickey Mouse stuffed doll.

"She then took your son to an abandoned warehouse somewhere near
Whittier Boulevard in East Los Angeles, where your brother waited for
her to arrive with the boy. But she didn't show up as scheduled. Your
brother was getting ready to search for her when he saw your son walking
around the area."

Michael lowered his head. Putting down the journal, the sheriff
looked directly at Gloria and Justin as he commented, "The rest happened
just like Detective Sergeant Kenyon of the L.A.P.D. reasoned it out a long
time ago." He turned to Michael again, and asked, "Do you know where
I can find this Cecilia Castro-Biddle?"

"Cecilia Castro-Biddle is my biological mother. She was an ...
emotionally unstable person. Apparently, she felt extremely guilty for
having given me up for adoption. That's how Soren Bjorgun was able
to convince her to kidnap me when I was four years old. I'm afraid
Paul also preyed on her emotions and used her for his own purposes. In
Mrs. Damasco's report you will see that Cecilia Castro-Biddle took her
own life about four months after my son's death."

"Your brother was quite a determined man," the sheriff remarked.

"Are we talking about a suicide or another homicide in the case of Cecilia Castro-Biddle?"

Michael shook his head, and said wearily, "I wouldn't know about that, sheriff."

"Mr. Cisneros, do you have any idea why your brother waited so long to complete his revenge? Justin inquired.

"I don't know the answer to that either, Mr. Escobar. Perhaps it has to do with the *Irmandade*'s business priorities. Perhaps as Mrs. Damasco said yesterday in my office, Paul couldn't really kill me directly. He could only destroy everything I ever loved ... . I really don't know, Mr. Escobar."

Although Gloria hadn't meant to stare at Michael, she had inadvertently found herself doing so, prompting him to smile reassuringly at her. She could tell that his soul like hers was walking in the pre-dawn of grief. She wondered how any of them would deal with the repercussions of the tragic events of the night before. The sedative had almost entirely worn off, and she felt as though her eyes as well as her nose and throat were on fire.

Noticing Gloria's gasping for breath, Otilia asked the sheriff if she could turn on an electric fan that was sitting on a filing cabinet. Justin also got up to give her a cup of coffee, holding it while she sipped. As a deputy handed Gloria the typewritten deposition, Justin took it instead and read it to her. Gloria signed the deposition, then looked into Justin's eyes. She saw the shadow of guilt and sorrow in them, and only then did she fully realize that Justin had killed a man the night before—the man who had killed Luisa.

Before anyone could stop her, she walked towards the door and headed out to the main road, moving faster and faster until she found herself running through misty fields of grapevines. She slipped and fell on the moist earth as her pain took hold of her eyes and mouth.

A moment later, she felt Justin's arm holding her up. "Sh. Sh. It'll be all right, I promise," he reassured her, as his lips brushed hers softly. Then she vaguely heard the sheriff say that the ambulance had arrived.

Justin lifted her up to the stretcher and helped the sheriff put her in the ambulance. An attendant took her pulse and pressure, then gave her a shot.

"Another sedative," Justin murmured close to her ear.

Her mouth felt strange, and she wanted to ask for a drink of water, but her lips couldn't begin to form the words.

As in a dream, Gloria felt herself floating, travelling down a road where very old eucalyptus and oak trees stood defiantly against the sky.

Then suddenly Luisa was there, running down a path flanked by acacias in bloom, saying something that Gloria couldn't hear.

There were people constantly talking to her in whispers, but she couldn't understand what they were saying. Someone held her hand for a long time. "Luisa?" Gloria asked. She heard someone reply, "I'm here." Somehow, Gloria knew it wasn't Luisa but her daughter Tania who had answered her. In her state of mind, she thought it was natural that Luisa and Tania should share the same voice. After that, she heard nothing and felt nothing. The pulsating darkness in her mind held neither fantasies nor dreams.